My W'

The *Kinky* Escort

Book Three

"Paid For His Services"

By JJ Stuart

Standard Legal Blurb

This is a work of fiction. All rights reserved. No part of this publication may be reproduced, distributed or transmitted in any form with prior written permission from the publisher, except in the case of brief quotations and reviews. All characters, names, places, and locations are fictitious. Any resemblance to persons living or dead is purely coincidental.
This work of fiction is intended for mature audiences.
Enjoy!

JJ Stuart © 2017

Table of Contents

"This book is dedicated to the age old male fantasy of impregnating beautiful fertile young women"

JJ Stuart

Three For One Deal

I don't know who was more nervous when we learned my wife was on her way up, Ashley, her two friends, Heather and Amy, or me. Veronica was escorted by one of the butlers to Ashley's private quarters, and I could tell the moment she stepped out of the elevator, that she had questions.

I got out of my chair and greeted my wife. She looked stunning in her scarlet red dress and matching gloves, but her eyes told another story. She glanced at me and then her eyes flickered towards the three women in the room. Her expression said *we need to talk.*

"You're back early," I said as I kissed Veronica's cheek. "I trust everything went okay?"

"Yes, everything was fine." Veronica's voice was neutral. "I completed my obligations and decided to teach young Steven a lesson. I'm done with him. How are you doing, *husband?*"

She was expecting Ashley and me, so I knew I had to explain the situation quickly. Part of me wanted to ask more about Steven and what she meant by being done with him. How did she teach him a lesson? What happened? First things first, though.

Turning towards Ashley, I got her attention. "If you don't mind, I'd like to discuss your new proposal with my wife, in private. Perhaps you could share the same with Amy and Heather?"

Ashley nodded. "We'll use my bedroom and chat in there."

"Thank you," I said as Ashley and her two friends eagerly shuffled out of the living room leaving me alone with my wife. I turned and smiled sheepishly.

Veronica waited until she was certain the young women were out of earshot. She crossed her arms – never a good sign – and tapped her foot – an even worse sign. "Care you explain what's going on?"

"I made a deal," I explained, hoping to forestall an outburst. "It's not final, or anything. I told Ashley that everything depends on the approval of all participants, including you."

"What kind of deal?"

"I agreed to Ashley's request that I try to impregnate her, but she was insistent I also agree to help Amy and Heather get pregnant too. I said I didn't work for free, and that I wasn't wild about having three children out of wedlock without first discussing the idea with my wife. That is why Ashley had you brought to us."

"What deal did you arrange?" Veronica said, her tone curious.

"I said if they paid me four-thousand-dollars each, then something could be arranged where we are all satisfied."

I could see Veronica chewing the numbers over in her mind. "So you would sire three children instead of just one." It was more of a statement than a question.

"Well, yes," I said. "That's the idea. Don't raise your eyebrows at me. I think their group impregnation idea is weird too. All I'm doing is providing a service for a fee I'm not going to be raising their children too. Look, they are all lesbians, and finding a surrogate to start a family is quite standard, I understand."

"I'm not sure I like this idea," Veronica said.

"You think I should have asked for more?"

"It's not that. It just bothers me that a part of you will be out in the world. Three parts of you. When are we going to start our family?"

I didn't know what to say. Veronica and I had talked at length about starting a family while she was a teacher. But after losing her job and my subsequent layoff, we had too much debt to think about raising kids. It wouldn't have been the responsible thing to do. Now, just as we were on the cusp of financial freedom, it only made sense to talk about having children again.

I had to say something. "I suppose once our debts are paid off, and we've saved up a nest egg; then we can talk about it. You won't be able to escort once we have kids. In essence, you'd retire. We'd have to find new jobs," I watched her reaction carefully.

"I'm not ready to give up escorting just yet," Veronica said. "It just bothers me that other women get to have your babies but I can't."

"If you want, I will tell them no deal, and we can go back to your room."

"I just don't like sharing you," she said. I saw her lip start to tremble, and I reached my arms out and hugged her. She held it together, and I was proud of her.

"Honey, our time will come. We're not going to be in this business forever."

"I know," Veronica said. She rested her head on my shoulder.

"I thought, with the money I make doing this, that we take a cruise vacation. Just you and me. What do you think?"

"A holiday?" Veronica asked her face lighting up. She wiped her cheek.

"I think we deserve a little vacation break. So you're game?"

Veronica answered by throwing her arms around me and planting kisses all over my face and neck. I laughed, unable to contain myself. I dug my fingers into her sides and tickled her, and Veronica shrieked with laughter. We wrestled and then kissed and continued to roughhouse until we heard the sound of someone clearing their throat.

I glanced up after pinning Veronica in a headlock and poking her sides. Her scarlet red dress rode up her legs exposing her white panties as she jabbed me in return. I released my wife, and she sat up, her long raven hair completely disheveled. She seemed startled to see Ashley and her two friends staring with wide eyes.

"Oh, you're back," Veronica said while brushing the hair from her face and pulling her dress down. She tried to act dignified and collected. "We were just talking."

"I take it your wife has agreed to the terms?" Ashley asked hesitantly. "Or were you two still negotiating?"

"Yes, she agreed," I said. "Are the terms acceptable to Heather and Amy as well?"

"They are," Ashley said with an amused smile. "Will you require payment now, or after the completion of your services?"

I glanced at Veronica. She cleared her throat. "Now would be preferable."

"Not a problem," Ashely said. "We will be back shortly with the funds. Cash is preferred, I assume or do you take cheques?"

"Cash would be perfect, thank you," Veronica said in a dignified voice.

"We will be back shortly," Ashley said. She gestured towards Amy and Heather, and the two girls followed her to the elevator. Neither girl said anything, and I wondered if they were having second thoughts, or were just nervous.

When the elevator closed and Veronica and I were alone, I turned to her and admired her natural beauty briefly. She was such a little firecracker. I was worried about what she had said regarding Steven and pondered how best to broach the subject.

"So, my love," I said casually. Her eyes turned towards me. "Remember that part you mentioned earlier about being done with Steven? Care to elaborate?"

Veronica dug into her purse and produced a tiny key.

I glanced at it. "Handcuff keys?"

"Yup. Remind me to give this to one of the cleaning ladies. Preferably whoever cleans Steven's private apartments."

I groaned. "What did you do now?"

"I cuffed him to the bed, and had sex with him."

"How was it?"

"Terrible. Steven's cock was so small I barely felt it. But it wasn't that. I was just tired of his attitude. He thought he owned me, and I gave him a little reality check. Just because you have paid for a service doesn't mean you own the person providing the service. People need to be civil and respectful. I informed the little twerp that I fulfilled my duties, and he will not be using my body anymore."

"And you left him cuffed to the bed?"

Veronica nodded. "So that he had time to reflect on his attitude."

I ran my hand through my hair and took a deep breath. "I hope Mr. Rutty doesn't take this the wrong way."

"I have a feeling Mr. Rutty doesn't think highly of his nephew. To me, people like Steven are parasites. All they do is take. At least Mr. Rutty is a gentleman."

I nodded in agreement. Veronica can be free spirited, and I could see her reacting exactly as she described. I cared nothing for Steven.

"You should probably pay Mr. Rutty a visit," I said. I considered for a moment and then added, "A few visits at least, and butter him up. He might be less inclined to be upset over how you treated his nephew if his cock is happy."

A little giggle escaped Veronica's lips. "Oh, I plan on doing that."

"So why are you so upset over this little side deal? You don't see me getting upset when you're with clients. I thought you would be happy I managed to earn some extra money."

Veronica thought for a moment. Then she leaned back on the couch and rested her hand on her head. "I guess I'm just not used to the idea of you having sex with other women. I'm not used to feeling jealousy. Is this what you feel every time I'm with a client?"

"What, jealous?"

"Yes."

"Sometimes. I felt jealous when you were with your co-worker. Mostly I'm just afraid you're going to run into the perfect guy one of these days and not want to be with me."

"I have the perfect guy," Veronica said.

"But I don't have a mansion," I said looking around the room. "Or fancy exotic cars, or a sailboat, or a summer home in Aspen. I mean, I'm an old ex-marine and unemployed firefighter. Sometimes I feel inadequate."

Veronica scampered across the couch and crawled into my lap. I loved when she did that. She was so small and compact; she fit perfectly in my arms.

"Listen you big lug," Veronica said, grabbing my chin with her hand and staring into my eyes. "I love you. No one can compete. I'm sorry I got a little jealous. I'm proud of you. Now get those girls pregnant. That's an order."

I had to laugh. As Veronica wrapped her arms around me and snuggled, an idea formed in my mind; a kinky kind of idea but one that had always been a fantasy of mine.

"Sweety," I said quietly.

"Yes?"

"I have an idea."

"That's never a good thing. What is it this time?"

I explained my fantasy idea to Veronica, and she listened first with amusement and then with interest on her face. By the time I finished, she was nodding thoughtfully.

"So what do you think?" I asked.

"I think I was wrong to think I was the kinky one in this relationship. Is this something you really want?"

"Every guy wants this. You don't have to, of course, but it would mean the world to me if you did."

"My oh my, I think I've created a kinky monster. If this fantasy means that much to you, then I'll do it. But you have to make sure Ashley and her friends are on board first."

My cock was already getting hard with anticipation. "If those three girls want to get pregnant, they'll be on board," I said. I could feel the heat on my face.

Three young women plus my wife? I've never had a foursome.

Veronica Takes Charge

Ashley, Heather, and Amy were sitting side-by-side on the couch watching as Veronica put their payment in her purse. Everyone seemed nervous, but I was probably the most nervous of all. With my wife present, I didn't feel so nervous. It's not every day a man is asked to impregnate three young women.

"So, is everyone okay with my idea?" I said to break the tension in the room. Everyone knew what was supposed to happen, but no one had any ideas on how to start the ball rolling.

"I'm definitely cool with it," Ashley said, turning towards her friends.

"I'm nervous, but if everyone else is okay, then I'm willing," Amy said. She was the timidest of the three girls. Her face nearly matched her red hair. I could tell she was nearly paralyzed with anxiety and would probably take the most convincing before she was ready.

I looked at Heather who was still thinking.

"I'm totally game," Heather said eventually. "Is your wife up for this?"

As if on cue, Veronica took the lead and stepped forward. She stood in the middle of the room, planted hands on her hips and surveyed the three young women peering up at her with disdain. The roleplaying had begun.

"What pathetic looking slaves," Veronica sneered. "I ask for breeding slaves, and this is what they send me? Useless, ugly whores not worthy of my breeding bull's attention. I have half a mind to send you back to the dungeons."

Amy's eyes became saucers while Heather grinned immediately. Even Ashley, once she got over her initial shock at my wife's words, seemed amused. Veronica paced back and forth, making sure she had the attention of all three women before she weaved her story further.

It has always been a fantasy of mine to have my wife roleplay a dominant. Often with clients, I weaved a similar fantasy for Veronica. Creating a fictitious scenario often breaks the ice for people and gives an enjoyable and safe framework in which to act out fantasies. Think of it like playing doctor as a child, except a whole lot kinkier.

"Are you slaves worthy of bearing children for Master?" Veronica asked in a menacing voice. There was no need to define who Master was. He could remain a nebulous figure in each girl's mind.

"Yes, Mistress," Heather replied quickly.

Amy glanced at her friend and mimicked her words. "Yes, Mistress."

Veronica turned towards Ashley and raised an eyebrow.

"Yes, Mistress," Ashley said. She was getting into it.

Spinning on her heel, her scarlet red dress perfect for her role, Veronica strode towards me. I waited with hungry eyes as my wife approached, ready for whatever her kinky mind conjured.

"You, Breeding Bull, stand up."

I obediently clamored to my feet and stood still. Veronica circled me, her eyes looking me up and down. It took an effort to keep my face straight.

"And this is the pathetic breeding bull they send me?"

I blinked in surprise, but Veronica was ready.

"Eyes forward," she snapped. "You are nothing but a breeder. You are lower than even these worthless slaves. Your job is to obey. Is that understood?"

"Yes, Mistress," I said meekly. My cock was hard, but I dared not touch it. Damn, I loved roleplaying.

Turning towards the girls, my wife looked stern. "You there," she said pointing towards Amy. "Take Breeding Bulls clothes off. Now."

"Yes, Mistress?" Amy replied in a cowed tone.

I remained passive, but I knew the corners of my mouth had risen. Amy looked at me and hesitated. Veronica wasn't having any of it.

"Are you hard of hearing, slave? Strip him!" Veronica barked again.

Scampering to her feet, Amy approached me. I could see the whites of her eyes and her flushed face told me she was embarrassed. I stood still. If I was playing the breeding bull, then I had to remain passive and only follow Veronica's instructions. If I helped Amy take my clothes off, I would ruin the illusion.

Reaching for the top button of my dress shirt, Amy fumbled with trembling hands. One by one she plucked my buttons and then slid my shirt off my shoulders. When Amy pulled my shirt off my shoulders, I watched her face and noted with pride that she was startled by my muscular chest abs. She sucked in her breath and paused for a moment, her eyes looking me up and down in a new light.

"Keep going slave," Veronica ordered, not amused by Amy's appraising eye.

"Yes, Mistress," Amy said. She reached for my belt buckle, and I could hear her breathing quicken as her neck and face flushed slightly. She pulled my belt through the hoops and dropped my pants to the floor. Peering up at me, Amy's eyes grew hungry. She grabbed my boxers and wiggled them down.I felt my cock spring to attention and knew every eye in the room would be looking at it.

Glancing at Veronica, I could see she was gauging the reaction of the three young women to seeing me naked. I couldn't tell what she was thinking, but part of me guessed she was sexually aroused. My wife was a kinky woman.

"You two," Veronica barked, pointing at Heather and Ashley. "Get up. I want all three of you to inspect the breeding bull. Put your hands on him. Touch him, rub him. Become familiar with his cock."

I suppressed a smile. I didn't mind three hot women inspecting my body, but I was hoping Veronica would have had them strip for me first. I felt strange being completely naked while everyone else was still clothed. So long as Veronica helped me to impregnate these three young ladies, I was willing to play along.

It was strange having so many admiring hands caress and touch my body while I looked at my wife. Veronica was enjoying herself and waited patiently as the three young woman swooned over me. When she had seen enough, she clapped her hands sharply, and all three women turned to look at her.

"I haven't decided which of you cows will be bred by my bull, so we will have a little competition. Get on your knees and open your mouths," Veronica said in a commanding voice.

Heather and Amy exchanged glances while Ashley eagerly knelt and opened her mouth. Without a word, they shrugged and knelt as well, eyes wide and their faces flushed. My cock tingled as I gazed at three upturned faces and warm, inviting mouths.

Veronica walked behind the three kneeling young women. "When the breeding bull stands in front of you, whoever services his cock with her mouth the best, will be judged worthy of being bred."

I could hardly wait. Veronica smiled at me and nodded. Stepping forward and pondered my options, I had the luxury of deciding which warm mouth would take my cock first. There was Ashley, of course, with her startling blue eyes and pretty face. I wanted to feel her mouth around my shaft. Then there was Heather, with her wildly styled short blonde hair and brown eyes. She was cute and looked very enthusiastic. Lastly was Amy, with shoulder-length red hair, a small freckled nose, and nervous blue eyes. I decided to start with Amy.

I planted myself in front of the kneeling redhead and tilted my cock down. There was something I found very arousing about Amy's timidness. I couldn't put my finger on it, but she was the one I wanted to fuck the most. What man didn't want to taste a redhead?

Seeing that she had to go first, Amy leaned forward on her knees. She glanced up at me, and then looked at my cock with a mix of fear and excitement. She then turned and looked at her friends, but Heather and Ashley were staring straight ahead.

"Eyes front, slave!" Veronica barked.

Amy immediately focused once more on my cock. I could feel the warm breath of her nervousness. She tentatively stuck out her tongue and licked the underside of my cock. She then kissed the tip. I wasn't in a rush and enjoyed seeing her hesitation. Half the fun was in the anticipation.

"His cock isn't going to suck itself, slave. Get to work," Veronica said.

I glanced at my wife and cringed. Part of me wished she would tone it down a little. I enjoyed watching Amy's timidness as she built up the courage to take my cock in her mouth. There was no need to rush the poor girl.

Amy opened her mouth and slipped my cock between her lips. Aside from Veronica, I had never been sucked off by another woman in my life, and it felt strange. With my wife watching, I relaxed and enjoyed the sensations of a new mouth around my cock. For all her nervousness, Amy's warm mouth felt great. She was gentle, and her tongue worked the underside of my shaft calmly. She couldn't take all of my length, but that was fine with me. After a few minutes of pleasure, I gently pulled out and thanked her with my eyes. I could get used to blowjobs from Amy.

Stepping sideways, I looked at Heather next. She winked at me. Rising on her knees, Heather quickly slipped my cock between her lips. Where Amy was slow and deliberate, Heather was quick and sloppy. I gasped as she took my whole cock at once, forcing herself to gag. Veronica was intrigued and stepped closer. She had never seen another woman suck me off, and I could tell by the intensity of her green eyes, that my wife loved it.

After a few minutes, I had to pull my cock from Heather's mouth to calm the tingling sensations. Otherwise, I would have climaxed. I'm normally not this trigger happy, but then again, I've never had three warm young mouths offering blowjobs. Heather sat back on her knees and fixed me with a perplexed expression. Perhaps she wondered if she displeased me. I dearly wanted to plaster her cute face with spunk, but I had a mission to finish and would be needing every last drop I could muster.

"I just need a moment to recover," I said raising a hand and willing my cock to calm down. I couldn't blow my load this early no matter how excited I felt.

"No rest Breeding Bull. Back at it, now!" Veronica ordered.

"Yes, Mistress," I said as I moved in front Ashley.

I just hoped Ashley was terrible at sucking cock. Otherwise, I feared I might accidently fill her mouth with cum. I stared down at her big blue eyes and watched her mouth open. I had to groan. She didn't seem the least bit timid. About half my cock was in her mouth before her warm lips sealed around my shaft and I felt her gentle tongue. I cringed and bit my lip; it felt too good. She pulled her head back and then moved it forward, taking nearly my entire length in one smooth motion. I gasped and clenched my fists. Why did she have to be so good? I needed all the sperm I could get to impregnate one of them.

Veronica watched in fascination as Ashley calmly moved her head back and forth, ignoring the saliva that soon trailed down her chin. She sucked with only one thought in her mind; to do better than her friends and be the first one impregnated.

I looked at my wife with a worried expression on my face. She glanced at me and then frowned and tilted her head. Suddenly understanding flashed on her face that I was about to orgasm.

"That is enough!" Veronica said, coming to my rescue.

Ashley calmly stopped sucking and sat back on her knees. A triumphant expression of smugness was on her face. She knew she had won. I feared the slightest stimulation would send me over the edge now. I didn't want to be humiliated in front everyone with a case of premature ejaculation.

Deep breaths, Jake.

As if reading my thoughts, Veronica strode down the line. She pivoted at the end, her scarlet dress hiding nothing of her beautiful figure. She tapped a gloved finger on her chin as if thinking. "I have observed your pitiful attempts at servicing cock, and I'm not impressed. If you were my slaves, I would have you all sent back to the dungeons and whipped."

I loved how Veronica so easily stepped into the role she was playing. I glanced at Ashley, Heather, and Amy and saw that they too were getting into the spirit of make-believe. Amy cringed when she heard my wife berate her. Heather, on the other hand, was smirking and eyeing my cock. It wasn't hard to decipher what was on her mind. Ashley, though, seemed the most confident as she stared ahead, her face unreadable.

"Based on your demonstration, I have decided who will be impregnated first," Veronica said. She strode down the line of girls once more, letting the suspense hang in the air and giving my poor cock some time to recover more.

I silently thanked my wife for the delay.

"I have decided that slave Ashley will be bred first," Veronica said. "On your feet slave, it is time to prepare your cunt for my bull. Slaves Heather and Amy will watch and assist. Move it!"

As far as I could remember, I've never been so aroused in my life, except possibly on my wedding night. I was about to have unprotected sex with a fertile, ovulating young woman, and then fill her womb with my spunk.

Could life get any better? Yes, it could; I was also getting paid.

Veronica had Ashley stand in front of the couch and turn to face me. She then placed Amy and Heather on either side and made them grab Ashly's arms tightly.

"Now, I'm going to pause the role playing for one moment," Veronica said as he held up a hand for silence. She made sure we all had looked at her before she continued. "Ashley, are you certain, that this is what you want? You understand that my husband is about to impregnate you with his sperm?"

Ashley glanced at her two friends, receiving reassuring nods in return. She looked at my wife with firm determination. "Yes, this is what I want."

"Very well," Veronica said. I appreciated my wife's forethought in making sure Ashley understood the ramifications of what was about to happen.

I remained silent, but inwardly I was very proud of my wife. It hadn't occurred to me to double check that consent had was given. I was suddenly very aware of the magnitude of the decision these girls were making, despite the fact that I was enjoying myself. These three young women all wanted to have babies; that was a life long commitment not to be taken lightly.

Clapping her hands, Veronica resumed her role as the dominant female. She pointed at Heather. "You, slave, hold Ashley's arms behind her back." Then, looking at

Amy, she said, "And you strip the clothes off this slave. Let's show my husband what succulent treasures await him."

I could see the startled expression on Ashley's face turn to a smirk as her wrists were wrenched and held behind her back. Amy suppressed a grin as she turned and began removing Ashley's clothing. It seemed to me that Amy was finally warming up to role playing.

It didn't take long before Ashley's clothes were off and she stood with both arms pinned behind her back by Heather. Amy scooped the clothes and tossed them aside while Veronica stepped closer to inspect her breeding slave.

I cleared my throat, and the four women looked at me like I had rudely interrupted a sacred moment. I shrunk back, indicating my cock was getting soft with a pitiful expression on my face.

"Oh, you'll be fine," Veronica said with a dismissive wave of her hand.

Amy covered her mouth and giggled.

"I'm starting to like your wife really," Ashley said to me.

I made a dejected, sad face. "Yeah, I get that a lot."

"Oh you big baby," Veronica said as she came over to me and patted my cheek. She winked and then slowly got onto her knees.

I gasped. Veronica's gloved hand gripped my semi-hard cock and gave it a few encouraging tugs. "Oh, my big baby is getting soft."

Saying nothing to ruin what she might do, I simply watched, as did the three girls behind her. With my cock growing harder, Veronica slipped it into her mouth and started to suckle and slurp. The sensations were all I needed, and within seconds I was rock hard again.

Pulling my cock out, Veronica dabbed the corners of her mouth and calmly gave me her hand. I gripped it firmly and helped her to stand.

"Thank you," she said. "We can continue now."

I could see the expressions on the other girls change from shocked curiosity to one of awe. Not only were they starting to like Veronica, but I think they were also starting to admire her too. I stroked my cock and admired my wife's backside for a moment before staring at Ashley's naked body before me.

"Time is wasting," Veronica barked. "Put this slave on her back here," she said pointing to the middle of the couch. "Arms under her backside and legs spread apart."

As if snapping out of their trance, Heather and Amy maneuvered Ashley onto her back, wiggling her torso until her ass was hanging off the edge. Then they both took one of Ashley's legs and sat on either side holding them steady. They were eager to watch their friend get fucked it seemed.

I came closer and admired Ashley's freshly shaven pink pussy so plump and swollen and fertile. My eyes traveled up her silky smooth stomach to her heavy bare breasts. Even on her back, Ashley's breasts were so firm they stood like round peaks, her nipples pointing straight up. Her startling blue eyes stared into mine. I could see the flush on her cheeks and neck as her breathing quickened. She opened her mouth and licked her top lip as her eyes focused on my hard waiting cock. That was all the invitation I needed.

Veronica knelt on the floor, the slit in her scarlet dress showing her shapely leg. She ran her velvet soft gloved hands up and down Ashley's inner thigh, caressing her creamy white skin.

I couldn't resist the urge to taste Ashley. I dropped to my knees beside my wife and crawled closer to Ashley's waiting pussy. My cock throbbed with anticipation. Veronica smiled at me. I started by kissing Ashley's soft inner thighs, working my way closer to her mound where I could feel the heat radiating from her glistening pussy.

Without a word I found my mouth hovering over Ashley's quivering vulva. I inhaled her musky scent and closed my eyes. I licked the length of her folds and tasted her hot liquid. I was in heaven. I latched onto her clit with my mouth and started to lick and suck her roughly. Ashley gasped, and I felt her body respond. I scooped my arms under her legs and lifted her bum. Ashley groaned and tried to bend her knees, but Heather and Amy held her firm. They were entranced with my performance.

A soft hand touched my shoulder. I opened my eyes and saw my wife's face next to mine. Her green eyes burned with desire. I set Ashley's bottom down and moved aside. Veronica moved in with hungry abandon and began to lap and suck Ashley's clit. I must have looked stunned because Ashley giggled. I looked at her, and she smiled at me seductively. I had never seen my wife go down on another woman and the sight was more arousing than I had ever imagined.

The effect must have been double on Ashley. She tilted her head back and released a long pleasurable moan. Veronica kept her mouth working, sucking and slurping Ashley's helpless pussy until the poor girl started to buck and grind. It didn't take long for my wife to bring Ashley to orgasm. All I could do was watch in fascinated rapture. I wasn't the only one. Amy was rubbing her clit, and Heather never blinked once.

"I think she's warmed up," Veronica said.

My wife's face never looked prettier, her lips and face glistening with Ashley's warm juices. Without thinking, I grabbed my wife and started to kiss her. I didn't want to waste a drop of Ashley's succulent nectar on my wife's face. Veronica wrapped her arms around my neck and returned my kisses with equal passion. As we kissed, my wife and I savored the taste between us.

Veronica would have continued making out with me, but I broke her embrace and pushed her aside. She gasped and rolled out of my way as I positioned myself between Ashley's legs and grabbed my throbbing cock. Working my shaft up and down her folds, I found Ashley's willing entrance and slipped in.

When I say Ashely was tight, that's an understatement. She was very tight, and her pussy gripped me like a vice despite her being so aroused. I worked my cock back and forth, amazed at her grip, while everyone watched with interest. It took no time for my cock to become slippery with Ashley's warmth. I finally sank into her, enjoying every sensation her pussy offered and listening to Ashley's soft moan.

With my cock fully inside of her, I leaned down and sucked one of Ashley's breasts for a moment. I then grabbed her upper thighs firmly. I gave her long rhythmic thrusts. Even though my job was simply to impregnate her, I wanted to enjoy her tight pussy. I might be the only man who ever fucks her, I thought, and it would be a crime not to enjoy myself for as long as I could.

At Veronica's suggestion, both Heather and Amy maneuvered beside Ashley's torso and started to fondle and kiss her breasts. I watched their faces kissing and licking and gasping and moaning and started to hump faster. I looked at Veronica and noticed she was watching me with interest.

"I love you," I whispered.

Veronica laughed and shook her head. She was more fascinated with watching my cock slip between Ashley's stretched pussy than watching the three girls kissing. Something about having my wife watching and the tightness of Ashley cunt made my cock tingle.

Oh, oh.

I was going to cum soon. There was nothing I could do. The situation was too taboo, and having my wife watching me was too thrilling. I held out for as long as I could, but my balls started pumping. I groaned and grabbed Ashley's legs even harder and started to power thrust my cock into her. Ashley cried out as she had an orgasm.

Seeing that I was close, Heather and Amy held Ashley's legs apart, their attention turning to my pistoning cock. Ashely ground her pussy into me and trembled. I continued with long deliberate thrusts until I gasped and rammed my cock all the way in just as my cock erupted deep inside her fertile womb. I could feel the force of the spurts. I held onto her legs as my balls pumped everything I had. I hadn't cummed so hard in years.

Exhausted, I waited with my cock still buried and caught my breath. No one moved. After a moment I slowly pulled my spent cock from Ashley's soaking wet pussy. Once I was out, my job was done, and I was brushed aside.

I watched as Heather and Amy helped spin Ashley around and set her butt on the back of the couch and held her legs up in the air.

"What are you doing?" I asked.

"They say if you do this right after sex for ten minutes, it doubles the chances of getting pregnant. Something about gravity," Heather said.

"Does it work?" I asked.

Amy and Heather shrugged.

I looked at Veronica dubiously, but she said nothing. I wondered if she was regretting her decision to allow me to impregnate Ashley. I was very aware of her desire for us to start our family. Discretion they say is the better part of valor, so I said nothing. It was better to leave her with her thoughts.

Scanning for my clothes, I found them and began to dress. As I was doing up my belt, Veronica silently appeared at my shoulder.

"How are you holding up?" I asked quietly so the three girls on the couch couldn't hear. They were still holding Ashley's legs in the air despite her protests to be allowed to stand.

"I'm okay. Did you enjoy that?"

"I wouldn't have if you weren't there," I said. "Thank you."

Veronica was quiet a moment, then patted my arm. "Well, it was the least I could do. You did a great job, husband."

It felt strange having my wife compliment me for trying to get another woman pregnant. Whatever her true feelings were, I knew Veronica well enough to give her some space to process her thoughts. I turned to survey the girls on the couch still balancing Ashley's naked legs in the air. It was almost comical.

"Well, ladies, I hope my performance was satisfactory," I said with a short bow. "My wife and I will leave you to it. If you don't mind, we are going to retire for the evening. It's been a very long day."

"When will it be our turns?" Amy asked with a worried glance at Heather.

"My husband will need a little time to recover, but I am certain he can accommodate you both tomorrow. For now, have a good rest, and thank you for a wonderful experience. Ashely, good luck to you too," Veronica said.

I offered my wife my arm and she gladly took it.

"Oh, I almost forgot the key!" Veronica suddenly said.

"The what?" I asked.

Veronica opened her slim purse and dug around for a moment before producing a handcuff key. She walked over to Ashley and held out her hand.

"What's this for?" Upside down Ashley asked taking the key from my wife.

"Your fiance will need these. I left him cuffed to his bed to think about his attitude towards women. You can rescue him now, or wait until the morning and give the key to the cleaning ladies. Either way, I am done with that boy. He is your concern now," Veronica said.

Ashley stared at the key for a moment before she started to laugh. "You mean to tell me that the man I'm unfortunately about to marry is handcuffed to his bed at this very moment?"

Veronica nodded.

"And this is the only key?"

Veronica nodded again.

"Oh, this is priceless. Are you sure Steven can't escape?"

"Not unless he can undo four pairs off cuffs using his cock," Veronica said. "And no offense, Ashley, but it doesn't reach that far."

"Don't I know it," Ashley grumbled. She winked and palmed the key.

I had a feeling poor Steven Rutty was going to be spending the entire night thinking about his poor life choices. With that done, Veronica and I both smiled and offered goodbyes once more. We walked towards the elevator and left the happy young ladies to some privacy.

I was beat. I could only imagine how tired my wife was. We said nothing while we waited for the doors to open. Just the silence of the moment was enough. A short time later we stopped outside of Veronica's room as she dug for her key.

"Do I have to sleep in my room?" I asked leaning against the wall and staring at the hallway ceiling.

Veronica unlocked the door and looked at me. "You're joking right?"

I laughed nervously and followed her into the room. "Of course I was joking. I'm sleeping with you tonight, my love."

"Damn right you are," Veronica said kicking the shut behind us with her foot.

A Well-Deserved Rest

The next morning I woke to the sound of knocking on the door. Daylight was streaming through a crack in the curtain. Who the hell gets up early on a Saturday morning and knocks on someone's door? I rolled over in bed and glanced at the bedside clock. It was nearly eleven o'clock.

Holy shit, I thought. I must have been tired. Veronica's side of the bed was empty. There was more knocking on the door, but I ignored it. Maybe they would go away. My wife appeared from the bathroom, showered and dressed. She glanced at me and then at the door while trying to fasten her watch. When it was clear that I wasn't getting up, she answered the door. A butler in a red-breasted suit bowed respectfully and handed Veronica a note. She thanked him and closed the door.

"What is it?" I asked half rolling onto my side and peering at her.

Veronica sat on the edge of the bed and opened the envelope. She read the note and then chuckled, before tossing it to me. I plucked the paper off the bedsheets, turned it right side around, and focused my eyes.

Dear Mr. And Mrs. Miller,

Seeing that you both have missed breakfast this morning, I assumed you were too tired for the morning activities too. I have taken the liberty of arranging a car to pick Mrs. Miller up at precisely one o'clock. Please pack appropriate summer wear and bathing suit. I shall be taking Mrs. Miller on a short pleasure cruise on my yacht with plans to be back for supper at five o'clock.

Please notify Mr. Miller that he will be spending the afternoon with my assistant, Ashley. She has informed me that Jake has expressed an interest in exploring the gardens and stables on the estate, so I have asked her to give a proper tour. Sorry for any inconvenience.

S incerel y,

H erbert Rutty.

"This is a joke right?"

"I don't think so. I guess I'm going for a boat ride," Veronica said.

I yanked the blankets and pulled them over my head. "Wake me up in an hour; I'm sleepy."

Veronica laughed and pulled my covers away. "Rise and shine. Lots to do today Mr. Grumpy. Get up. Shower, shave and get ready. I'm starving."

"Tell them we quit. I want to sleep more."

Lying on the bed beside me, Veronica poked my head with her finger. I didn't move. She poked again, making tiny popping sounds followed by, "Get up."

I could only tolerate her cuteness for so long. "Fine, I'm up. Stop poking me."

"Wear your navy polo shirt today and those white shorts," Veronica said.

Getting out of bed I stood on unsteady legs.

"Get in the shower old man. You have two young ladies expecting to get pregnant today, and you better not disappoint them," Veronica stated. "I have a reputation to uphold."

"Yes yes, I'm getting into the shower," I mumbled as I shuffled towards the bathroom. "It's always about the sex with you. Hurry up and shower, gotta have more sex, blah blah. Gotta gets more girls pregnant. I'm a person damn it; I'm not a piece of meat!" I slammed the bathroom door in jest.

I could hear Veronica's laughter on the other side of the door, and despite being tired, I couldn't help but laugh too. Being able to laugh together is the secret to a great marriage. Oh, and my ten-pound cock.

A Three Hour Cruise and a Monkey Wrench

By one o'clock, Veronica and I were waiting near the front steps of the mansion. She was carrying a small bag containing her bathing suit, lotion, a change of clothes and a small makeup case. Because she was going to be on a boat, Veronica had spent the better part of half an hour braiding her waist length hair. She looked younger with her hair pulled back, and her eyes looked even larger. For her boat ride, she decided on her cargo shorts, flip-flops and a pink tank top that clung to her full breasts. I had to admit she looked pretty hot. I made her promise to wear sunscreen and not fall overboard.

I was just wearing my navy blue polo shirt, white shorts, and sandals. I was pouting that no one wanted to take me on their fancy yacht. Though I was a little miffed, I understood Mr. Rutty's motives. He wanted some time alone with my wife without me being a cock-block. I got it.

Besides, I had my own problems to face. I was hoping to finish up my impregnation duties, but with Veronica stepping out of the picture to take a cruise, I would be flying solo. I wondered if I should wait until after dinner to try impregnating one of the girls. Would my wife mind if I worked without her? Sure, Veronica said she was fine with me fulfilling my obligation, but was she fine? I had to be very careful in feeling out her mood. In the meantime, we waited for Mr. Rutty's car to arrive and pick Veronica up.

"Ahh there you two are," said a familiar voice from behind us.

Veronica and I turned to see Ashley smiling at us. She looked radiant. I watched with amusement as my wife clapped her hands together and rushed over to Ashley. She threw her arms around the young woman and hugged her. Ashley, unsure of how to respond, peered at me hesitantly before returning my wife's hug.

"You get used to it," I said.

"So you do you feel?" Veronica asked. I couldn't tell which of the two was more excited, though I would bet at the moment, my wife was a smidgen ahead.

"I slept like a baby," Ashley said, then cupped her mouth and laughed. "I'm sorry I didn't mean to make a pun."

Veronica laughed. "Now, in a day or two you be sure to take one of those tests. I want to know right away if it worked."

"Honey, let the poor girl breathe. She'll be fine," I said.

As if on cue, a black limousine pulled to a stop. We all turned and watched a young chauffeur step out. He wore one of those caps you see chauffeurs in movies wear. I didn't think people wore those in real life. He stopped just short of the curb and bowed.

"I am here to escort Mrs. Miller to the yacht. If you have any luggage, I can store it for you, ma'am." The man had a French accent.

I turned towards my wife who was patting Ashley on the arm and saying her goodbyes. Mimicking a stuffy English accent, I said, "Yes, Darling, did you remember to bring the luggage? This good 'old chap is going to store it for you before he drives you to the yacht. Don't mind me. I'll just stay here and eat crumpets and drink tea."

"Oh stop being so rude," Veronica scolded me with a grin. She lowered her voice and leaned close. "Now trust me, everything is fine. Getting Heather and Amy pregnant is more important than my feelings so enjoy yourself. I'll be fine darling, I promise."

I sighed and nodded. "It's going to be weird without you there."

"Nonsense," Veronica said. She kissed me on the cheek and pointed the chauffeur towards her bag. The man bowed and put her one bag trunk of the giant stretched limo.

I stood forlorn. Ashley came and stood beside me, her arms folded under her ample breasts. She wore a beautifully tight pair of jeans and a blue turtleneck. We waved as Veronica giggled and hopped into the back of

41

the limo. The driver tipped his hat towards Ashley and I before getting in. We watched the big, sleek car wheel down the laneway and disappear.

"I hope she has fun," I said.

"With Mr. Rutty, she will. Trust me," Ashley said. "Come on let's go inside."

We walked back into the mansion. It looked like it was going to be a perfect day for sailing, or exploring gardens and horse barns, hurray.

"Aren't you going to be too hot in a turtleneck?" I asked.

"I thought it was going to be cooler."

"How do you feel today? No weird feelings?"

Glancing at me, Ashley tilted her head. "Like what? Morning sickness?"

I laughed. "That wasn't what I meant. I mean, no regrets? You aren't yelling and hitting me, so I assume you're okay with last night?"

"Aren't you?"

I was quiet for a moment. Ashley and I stopped by the elevator leading to her apartments. It wasn't until we were inside and headed up that I spoke again.

"To be honest with you, I felt a little weird. I've never gotten a girl pregnant before. Not even my wife. So the idea of trying to get you and your two friends pregnant–"

"Just felt strange?" Ashely interjected.

"Yeah, strange is a good word for it. First of all, it was flattering. I mean, of all the guys you rich girls could choose, I don't know why you decided on me."

Ashley blushed. When she saw I was waiting for her to say more, she covered her mouth with the back of her hand nervously.

"What is it?" I asked.

"Well, it was partly convenience. I mean, timing my pregnancy with this rite of passage for my fiance, then timing sex with him so it would look like your baby was his—"

"Yes, it's all very dizzying. But that's not what I meant. I mean why me? Why did you and your friends pick me?"

"Look at yourself," Ashley said. "Ex-Marine, big and buff. Nice ass. Good personality, kind and thoughtful. I mean sure you have a small cock, but—"

"What?"

"I'm kidding. Your cock is beautiful," Ashley said with a snort of laughter.

"Okay, I was beginning to worry there. Don't give me a complex."

"My fiance has a small cock. It's so depressing."

Our elevator came to a stop, and the doors slid open. I followed Ashley out and saw the now familiar living room and couch from the night before. Her friends were gone, which surprised me. I was expecting them to be waiting for us.

"So why are you marrying him?" I asked as I followed Ashley into her bedroom. It was a nice room, but I didn't care for pink walls and bed covers. It looked too much like a little girl's room.

I guess she saw my expression. "Oh, sorry. This was once someone else's apartment. They had a daughter who stayed in this room. I didn't have it redecorated because I'm marrying Steven so soon, I didn't want to bother."

I nodded. It made sense. Ashley lifted the hem of her shirt and peeled it off.

"Oh, I'm sorry," I stammered, stepping back and shielding my eyes with my hands. "Do you want some privacy while you change? I'm so sorry; I wasn't thinking."

Ashley stared at me. I lowered my hands and peered over the top of my fingers at her bewildered face.

"What the hell are you doing?" Ashley asked.

"You're changing your top. I thought I should look away. I can wait over—"

"Jake," Ashley said firmly as if trying to snap me out of a dream.

I looked at her. "Yes?"

"You just fucked the shit out of me last night. You ate my pussy. You've seen me naked twice. I've sucked your cock. Do you think I'm suddenly shy to change my shirt in front of you now?"

I blinked. She was right. I'm so stupid.

"Anyway, you asked why I'm marrying him? It's a long story. I'll explain it to you on our way to the horse stable. Do you ride horses, Mr. Miller?"

"No never."

Ashley paused and stared at me. "Seriously?"

I shook my head. "Was that a requirement?"

"Damn it," Ashley said. She starting flinging shirts out of her drawer until she found a dark red one she liked. She unfolded it, put her arms through and slipped it over her head angrily.

"Is something wrong?" I asked.

Taking a deep sigh, Ashley nodded. "Sort of. I should have checked first. Heather had a silly damsel in distress fantasy idea. She and Amy put costumes on and rode ahead of us. They've already left. We were supposed to ride through the woods, and you were supposed to find Heather and save her from Amy and then have wild passionate sex."

"I don't follow. This is role playing obviously," I said.

"Heather is dressed as a fair lady, with an old fashioned dress and costume jewelry. Like those women in the Jane Aire stories. Amy has a buccaneer costume and is playing the rogue bandit who kidnaps her. You and I were supposed to ride out to a clearing about an hour from here and rescue the fair maiden and then you were to fuck her silly on a blanket. There's a spring-fed pond there and a waterfall we were all going to swim in after. It's all romantic. Don't look at me; it was her idea."

"Ride for an hour?"

"We planned on being back by supper. Granted, Heather did want to be certain we had privacy to skinny dip a little. But because you don't know how to ride a horse, and I don't have time to train you, we will have to improvise. I can't leave them stranded and waiting."

I didn't like the sound of the word 'improvise.'

"I could ride a horse with you on the back, but not for an hour. No, there has to be a better idea. Damnit," Ashley said as she sat on the edge of her pink bed.

"Does anyone around here have a four wheel drive jeep?"

Ashley smiled. "As a matter of fact, yes. Hurry. You need to put on your dashing, handsome man costume."

"My what?" I didn't have a handsome man costume, whatever that was.

"Your costume. You can't rescue a fair maiden in distress and then have your way with her dressed in a t-shirt and shorts. Dressing up is part of the experience. You need to look like a dashing hero."

I should have asked for more money, I thought.

"Okay, fine," I said. "But I don't have a costume."

Ashley grinned, her startling blue eyes are wide with excitement. "Follow me. I have a costume Herbert wore last year at the pirate ball. You're about the same size as him, so it should fit you. Sorry for the rush."

There are things you do in the escort business that no one ever warns you about. This is one of them. I took a deep sigh and followed Ashley out of the bedroom. She was positively bouncing across her apartment with excitement.

"There better not be any funny hats," I called after her. "I hate funny hats."

A Little Cosplay Anyone?

"I also hate frilly shirts," I said while looking at myself in the mirror. I turned my body one way and then the next. The painted wooden sword was a nice touch, as were the leather pants and long boots. But I didn't care for the frilly white shirt.

"You look dashing," Ashley said.

"Why don't you have to wear a costume, Ashley?" I asked looking at her.

"Do you want me to?"

"Well if I have to look ridiculous, then it's only fair that you suffer too."

Ashley giggled and thought for a moment. "Well, I can't wear my ladies dress from the pirate ball. I don't want to steal the moment from Heather. I have some tight leggings, and oh, I had that elven archer outfit from cosplay last year! Yes, I could be your faithful squire."

"What is cosplay?" I asked, genuinely confused.

"It's like a comic book convention. People dress up in superhero costumes. Last year I went with Amy as elven warriors. It was lame, but we had a good time. Anyway, I still have the costume somewhere."

I watched as Ashley, skipped out of the room and back across her apartment. She had completely transformed from the stuffy blonde "assistant" I met just a day ago into a bubbly vivacious young woman. I had to remind myself that I have only known Ashley for a day. And yet I felt completely at ease around her. It was odd. Perhaps seeing a woman naked a few times, and then having wild passionate sex, does tend to knock down a few barriers.

I returned to the couch and waited while Ashley rummaged through her closet. I could hear her running commentary and smiled to myself. I guess there were worse ways to spend a weekend than dressing up as a pirate and having sex.

When Ashley returned holding a crumpled pile of green cloth, I was doubtful. Once more, without thought or embarrassment, Ashley began to peel off her clothes. This time I didn't look away. I wasn't sure if it was appropriate to admire her young body and ample breasts, but there was nothing else in the apartment to gaze at. Hopping on one foot and then the other, Ashley put her green leotards on. Then she fastened a very skimpy forest green miniskirt around her waist. Her top was simply a forest green bra with gold tassels and a shiny silver vest that left her midriff bare. Next, she donned brown leather boots up to her knees and a tiara sparkled with fake green emeralds in her hair.

"How do I look?" Ashley asked after giving me a twirl.

"Not bad. Will anyone say anything if they see us leaving the mansion like this?" I asked.

"I dunno, maybe. Who cares, right? Let's go rescue that poor maiden."

Together we took the elevator back down to the main floor and then walked out of the front doors of the mansion. Ashley led me around the side of the building, which was a long walk. There we descended a series of steps and walked along endless rows of flowers. I couldn't believe how much property Mr. Rutty owned.

"Oh, these are the gardens, by the way. So that you know," Ashley said without slowing her pace. She looked tasty in her elven outfit, and I once more admired her long legs. She was going to be a cool mom someday, I thought.

We continued past the gardens and down another short road towards the stables. I could see rows of buildings, and horse trailers, and pickup trucks. Someone around here had to have a jeep we could borrow. At least that was Ashley's plan.

Stopping in front of the main building Ashley walked into the office while I discreetly waited outside. I could hear voices inside discussing something. A half ton pickup slowly drove past and the driver glanced at me and shook his head. I gave him a nod and waved a frilly sleeved arm at him.

When Ashley came out of the office, she wasn't smiling.

"No jeep?" I asked, reading her expression.

"No. But we can use one of the old dirtbikes. Can you ride a motorcycle?"

I made that confident sound all men make when asked a silly question regarding innate abilities. Of course, I could ride a motorbike. She led me to the storage shed, and together we tried the rusty deadbolt and opened the door. We found the dirt bike under a tarp covered in bird droppings. I pulled it off, to spare Ashley's dignity and tossed the tarp aside.

Standing side by side, Ashley and I stared at the oldest motorcycle either of us had ever seen. It was pale yellow and covered with a layer of dirt and cobwebs. The long black seat was cracked, and the foam looked as if a mouse had used it for nesting material. It had seen better days. I looked at Ashley.

"It's either this or we double on horseback," she said.

I grabbed the bike and wheeled it backward out of the shed. Once outside, I checked the fuel and oil levels. Both seemed fine. I primed the engine clicked the gear shifter into neutral and kicked the starter. She blurted a loud protest but didn't start. I cranked the throttle a few times then waited a second. I put my foot on the kick starter once more and jumped down on it with all my might.

The engine sputtered then coughed, but she caught. Bluish smoke billowed out of the tailpipe. After a few revs of the throttle, she started to purr. I turned the choke down a little as the bike warmed up.

"Is it ready to ride?" Ashley asked looking at me dubiously.

"Do they have helmets?" I asked.

Ashley shrugged and walked back into the shed. After a quick look around she came out with her hands out to the side. No helmets. I pumped the throttle a little more and turned the choke off. It surprised me how well the bike ran.

I kicked my leg over the seat and flipped the kickstand. I gave the engine a few revs and looked at Ashley. She stepped closer, and I could tell she was nervous.

"It's easy," I said. "Just keep your feet on the back pegs, and don't touch the exhaust with your legs. Wrap your arms around my waist. When I lean, you lean. There is nothing to it. Hop on!"

She seemed encouraged by my words and cautiously mounted the bike. I felt her feet searching for the foot pegs briefly. I could feel her heavy breasts pressed into my back and I smiled privately.

"Ready?" I said over my shoulder.

"Don't do anything reckless."

I laughed, pulled in the clutch and popped the bike into gear. I gave it a bit of throttle and released the clutch slowly, and we were off. I quickly checked the front and back tires to see if they need air. Nope. I slowly accelerated and then changed to second gear. For an old bike, she ran smoothly. I was impressed.

"Okay, which way do we go?" I asked maintaining a slow roll across the yard.

Ashley pointed over my shoulder. "Follow this trail until I tell you to turn."

That was all I needed to hear. I revved the engine, and we gathered speed quickly. It was a peppy dirt bike and my memories of riding as a kid flooded back. It's true, what they say; you never forget how to ride a bike.

We had ridden for nearly twenty minutes before Ashley tapped my shoulder and I slowed the bike. We had gone down into the woods quite a way. I was thankful for the marked riding trails as it allowed me to enjoy the gorgeous scenery. Mr. Rutty owned some prime real estate with hardwood trees and gently rolling hills. It was a beautiful country, and I could see why Heather wanted to play out her fantasy within the magic of the forest.

"I think we're close. You should find a place to park. We can walk the rest of the way," Ashley finally said.

I nodded and slowed down even more. There was clearing beside the trail that looked like the perfect spot. The bike performed flawlessly, and I patted her fuel tank in appreciation as I cut the engine and the silence of the forest flooded in. Ashley climbed off and took a few bowlegged steps before straightening her back. I lowered the kickstand and gently leaned the bike over before stepping off.

"That was fun," I said. "Your hair looks like shit."

Ashley touched her head and felt her windblown blonde hair and laughed. She looked so different from the woman I had only met a day before. Her eyes were still startlingly blue, but her long blonde hair was all over the place, and she looked much better in an elf outfit than a dress.

"Well you don't look so handsome either," Ashley said. " I'm lying. You look hot. Okay, let's focus."

I laughed. Once Ashley had patted her hair down she grabbed my hand and led me back onto the trail, we had been riding down. It felt good to walk, but I felt a little strange holding her hand. She probably meant nothing by it, so I pretended I didn't notice. The trail rose slightly and opened into a little meadow. Ashley stopped and looked around. She seemed to be undecided.

"Please tell me you aren't lost," I said.

"Nope, but I think we rode too far. Yes, we did. It was before the meadow. We need to backtrack. Sorry."

I shrugged. It didn't bother me at all. I gave our surroundings one last glance then turned and followed Ashley back down the trail. She had let go of my hand either consciously or unconsciously and scouted ahead.

A short distance down the trail, the sudden movement to my right caught my eye. There was a person moving between trees, but I couldn't make out any details. My Marine training kicked in, and I grabbed Ashley by the arm and placed my hand over her mouth just as she was about to shriek. Her eyes were wide with fright for a moment, but I hushed her and pointed. I made it clear to stay low and not make a sound. When she nodded, I released my hand from her mouth and moved slowly towards the figure I had seen in the bush. They had taken cover. Turning my head back, I made eye contact with Ashley and gave her a hand signal to stay put. She nodded, and I carefully crawled over a fallen log and into the thicker parts of the woods.

I hunched low and peered into the trees, using my eyes and ears to detect any anomalies. A bird chirp, a twig snap, a crunching leaf under a boot. Any of those would be a sign that would give me a direction to focus on. A few moments later my first clue came. A twig snapped off to my left. I slowly swiveled my head, glad that my pirate outfit blended somewhat with the browns of the forest, except the frilly white pirate shirt.

A head poked around a tree about twenty feet away and then was gone. It was too quick for me to recognize any facial features. Then it poked around the other side of the same tree and disappeared again. The figure had red hair, and I smiled as I watched Amy moving to new cover.

"Amy I see you," I called in a loud voice.

The figure stopped, and I could see her arms pumping in frustration, then she crouched low and dropped out of sight behind the thicker brush.

"You are terrible at hiding. I totally saw you. Come out Amy," I shouted.

"I am not Amy!" Amy declared in a loud voice as she suddenly jumped to her feet. "I am Lady Waife bandit queen of Sherlock Forest! Engarde!"

I blinked in amazement as Amy drew a wooden sword and came running at me, bouncing over sticks and bushes and even a fallen log. She was surprisingly athletic, and I admired her grace. Perhaps I admired her body a little too long.

"Oh shit," I said and got to my feet. I ran towards Ashley who looked at me with wide eyes as I approached. She saw Amy for a moment before laughing.

"A sword? I need a sword. Where is it?" I asked frantically.

"I gave you one. Where did you put it?"

"I don't know!" It wasn't on my belt. It must have fallen off while we rode.

"Grab a stick or something; she's nearly here. We have to defend ourselves!"

Great. I had to find a stick while a crazed redhead was charging at me. Looking around I spotted a short stick and quickly picked it up. It would have to do.

I turned and faced Lady Waife bandit queen of Sherlock Forest or whatever she called herself. I was pretty certain it was supposed to be called Sherwood Forest, but I could be wrong. I raised my stick sword and prepared to do battle.

Amy came to a skidding halt and looked at me.

"Nice shirt," she said.

"I hate it."

"Me too."

"Where's your sword?" Amy asked.

I held up my stick, and she raised an eyebrow. "That's not a sword."

"Yes, it is," I said.

"No, it's not. That is a stick."

"Well, I lost my sword. This will have to do."

Amy scoffed. "We might be role playing, but you will lose. I'm a trained sword fighter."

"In real life?"

Amy nodded, a grin spreading across her cute face.

I looked at my stick and then at her wooden sword. "I'm fucked aren't I?"

Amy nodded again. "Why are you still smiling?"

"Because I know something you don't know," I said.

"Are we in that princess movie now, and this is where you tell me you aren't left handed?" Amy asked with a roll of her eyes.

I gaped. "You know that movie?"

Amy's laughter filled the forest. "Everyone knows that movie."

"Inconceivable," I said.

Holding her sword pointed at me, Amy's face became serious. "Drop, your, sword."

"I think you're bluffing," I said, quoting the movie.

"I might be, you vomitous monstrosity. But then again, maybe I'm not."

I couldn't keep the smile off my face. I looked down and tossed my stick to the ground. Amy stepped closer; triumph painted on her face. In a flash, I reached up and flicked the wooden sword from Amy's hand, caught it in mid-air and pointed the blade at her.

"Amazing," Amy said in complete disbelief.

I was about to bow when she turned and bolted into the woods.

Shit.

I looked over my shoulder at Ashley in dismay.

"Well go get her!" Ashley cried flinging her hands wildly.

I immediately gave chase, but Amy was quick and had a head start. I could see her ducking easily around branches and logs with her long slender legs. Amy was built for running. With nothing but determination, I barreled after her with considerably less grace. I wasn't sure how long I chased Amy through the woods, but I wasn't getting any closer.

"Come back here you wayward scoundrel!" I shouted. "Tell me where the fair maiden is!"

Amy glanced back and saw her lead. She grinned and shouted her defiance at me. "The bandit queen never gives up her captives! You will have to fight me to the death first!"

I resumed the chase and soon entered a clearing. I spotted Heather and Ashely casually sitting on a picnic blanket looking at me. Confused I came to a stop and looked at them.

"How did you get here so fast?" I said, my breathing labored.

"I took the path silly," Ashley said pointing behind her.

"Fuck me; there's a path?" I said, resting my hands on my knees and catching my breath.

"Of course there is. Why you took the hard way is beyond me. Anyhow carry on, our fair maiden here needs rescue," Ashley said.

"Hi, Heather," I said between breaths.

She smiled and nodded.

"Nice dress by the way. It shows your bosom off perfectly."

"Um, shouldn't you be fighting the evil bandit queen?" Heather asked.

Fine. I stood straight and wiped the sweat from my brow. Glancing around the clearing, I looked for Amy, but she was nowhere to be found. I did a full circle and then scratched my head.

"She appears to have fled. Or perhaps a giant dragon has eaten her." I turned to face Lady Heather and knelt on one knee. Stretching my arms outward I loudly professed my victory. "You have been rescued fair lady," I said, "Let's fuck."

I then noticed Heather and Ashley's head swivel to my right at the same moment. My years of military service told me this was not a good thing. I turned my head just in time to see Amy launching herself at me from a full run. I could have sworn a minute ago the forest was empty.

Luckily I've been in this exact situation with Veronica many times. I'm not sure if it's my charm or if there is just something about me that makes women want to run into me at full speed, but I was prepared.

Pivoting on my knees, I twisted my body and grabbed Amy's arm. Her expression changed from triumph to shock. I pulled her arm down and rolled my shoulder into her torso, using her momentum to carry her body harmlessly over mine and onto the ground.

I had the upper hand now. Without thought, I dove on top of Amy, but she was far from out of the fight and somehow counter rolled under my grasp. I ate a face full of leaves but I hooked her legs with my foot, and she sprawled. I swung around on my knees and made a grab for her even as she was clamoring to her feet once more. I got a hold of her spandex pirate queen pants and watched as they slid down her legs and caught around her bandit boots. She was wearing thong panties and the sight of her bare legs and gorgeous little ass momentarily froze me.

Yummy!

Amy gasped and cried out as she scampered and pumped her legs away from me. She got to her feet and somehow got one pirate boot off. I smiled and slowly got to my feet. She was as good as caught now. Amy hopped backward, her eyes wide aa she yanked the other foot off leaving just her pirate queen tunic, vest, and white panties as her only clothing.

"Surrender pirate queen!" I shouted in triumph.

61

"Never!" Amy shrieked with laughter. She picked up a stick and hurled it at me then turned and started to run. I was starting to like this girl.

I looked at Heather and Ashley, and they were both laughing hysterically. Picking up Amy's spandex pants and boots I shook my head. That girl had spirit.

"Go get her!" Heather shouted. "You have to defeat her before you can rescue me you dolt! Go!"

I wasn't getting paid nearly enough for this. I tossed Amy's clothes aside and began my pursuit once again. It wasn't hard seeing a pair of white legs running through a hardwood forest, so I had a much easier time tracking her this time around. I saw her dive over a fallen log and lay on the ground to hide. Now I had her. When I reached her hiding spot, Amy wasn't there. For a moment I was confused, but then I saw disturbed leaves on the ground and deduced that she had scurried down the embankment and had used the cover of the low ditch to continue running. Sneaky girl.

How long was I supposed to chase her, though? Sitting down on a log I decided to take a break. I had to catch my breath. I wasn't an eighteen-year-old Marine anymore.

The crunch of leaves behind me was my only warning. I felt Amy grab me from behind and pull me off the log. My legs kicked up into the air as I fell backward and landed hard. Amy laughed and started to pull my shirt. I felt buttons popping off and then one of my frilly arms tore clean off.

I stood and looked at my torn shirt in dismay. Amy was ten feet away, her shapely legs both alluring and quick. I pointed my finger at her. "You snuck up on me. I'm impressed."

"You look better without that shirt," Amy replied. "I'm impressed too."

"I don't understand you at all Amy," I said pulling the remains of my shirt off and tossing it aside. The warm summer air felt cool against my sweating skin.

Amy unbuttoned her pirate vest and slipped it off her shoulders and dropped in on the ground before tilting her head and regarding me with her piercing blue eyes. "What about me don't you understand?"

I looked at her bare legs and white panties. She didn't strike me as the thong type. I bent one leg over my knee and pulled my leather boot off. "I thought you were the timid one of the group. You seem like a completely different person today."

"Do I?" Amy said. She began to undo the buttons on her tunic.

"Yes," I replied switching my leg and pulling off my other boot. "If I were a betting man, I'd say you're the wild one in the group."

Amy's shirt fell to the forest floor. "And are you a betting man?"

"That depends on what the prize is," I said as I stood and unbuckled my pants.

"Oh, you're a man who likes rewards?" Amy asked. She stepped closer and unfastened her bra. Her breasts weren't large or heavy, but they suited her slender body perfectly. She watched my reaction carefully as I gazed at her bare chest.

I let my pants fall around my ankles. "I'm running out of lines to use here," I said. Amy squinted her nose and laughed. Maybe it was the way the sunlight made her red hair so bright, or how incredibly white her pale skin was, I don't know. All I knew was my cock was growing hard.

"Shouldn't we get back to Heather and Ashley?" Amy said, reverting to the timid girl I knew the night before. She seemed a little self-conscious.

I dropped my boxers and took a step closer, completely naked. Amy looked at my cock and then through the woods in the direction of the clearing. Heather and Ashley were a good distance off. Unless they had followed Amy and me, there wasn't a chance we would be found.

"What if they get mad?" Amy asked. She crossed her arms in front of her breasts and bit her thumbnail.

"Let them get mad," I said and moved closer. "It's your choice."

Amy peered at my face. She seemed to hesitate for a moment, but then she placed her hands on my chest.

"You're so strong," Amy said.

"You're so tiny," I replied.

"I've only had sex once. With a guy, I mean," Amy blurted. "Oh gosh, please don't hate me, but I don't like men."

Her revelation seemed strange to me, considering our situation. I put my hands on her slender shoulders and tucked a strand of red hair around her ear. "You don't like men?"

Amy shook her head as she lightly traced her fingers across my chest. "Not at all. Men are crass and rough. I like women much more."

Slipping my fingers through her hair, I tilted her head back. Her blue eyes searched mine, and she made a tiny gasp as I drew her closer and kissed her lips. As I held her head cradled in my hands Amy's hands slid downward and grasped my cock. It felt nice, and I responded by kissing her harder.

"Some men can be rough," I said between kisses.

"No more talking," Amy whispered. She was tugging and yanking on my cock while she kissed me.

I released my hold on her head, slid my arms under hers and lifted Amy off the ground. Her pale white legs hooked around my torso as her arms cradled my face.

She was a little higher than me now and kissed my forehead. I twined my fingers together across the small of her back and held her.

"Fuck me, please," Amy begged as she played with my hair.

I didn't say a word as I lowered her. She reached between her legs and found my cock. She guided me into her as I carefully lowered her body. When I felt the tip stab her hot pussy I held her steady for a moment. Amy wrapped her arms tightly around me and started to gyrate her hips into me. I very carefully lowered her more and felt the extreme pleasure of her tightness gripping my cock. Now it was my turn to be shocked as pleasure coursed through my entire body.

I moved my hands to cradle her ass and began to lift her up and down. She didn't weight much at all, and I could feel her lithe legs helping me with the effort. She placed her hands on my shoulders and arched her back and letting her red hair hang as she moaned and gyrated her hips into me.

It didn't take long for my cock to start tingling, but I didn't want to cum yet. I needed a pause to regain my endurance. As Amy slid down my shaft once more, I held her impaled. She opened her eyes and looked at me questionably. I smiled and carefully bent my knees. She held me tightly, keeping herself firmly on my cock as I slowly settled to the ground and laid on my back. Her legs unwrapped from my torso, and she planted her feet on the leafy ground. She was now squatting on top of me. I caressed her perky breasts and rolled her hard nipples between my fingers.

She leaned forward, her face wild with excitement. "Are you giving me control?"

I smiled and laughed a little. "You have vanquished me, rogue bandit queen. You may claim your prize. I can fight you no more."

I liked Amy's laughter. It reminded me of tinkling bells. She planted her hands on my chest and rose on the balls of her feet. While staring into my eyes, she lifted her bottom slowly, drawing a long pleasurable sigh from my lips. Her pussy, like Ashley's, was a warm vice. She then lowered herself and moaned like a huntress.

Folding my arms behind my head, I admired the rise and fall of her perky breasts as Amy lost herself in riding my cock. I knew I wouldn't last long and gave up fighting. I simply watched the sunlight streaking across her sweaty body and tried to remember the various contortions of her face as she bathed in the pleasure she felt. I don't know how many times she climaxed, but I counted at least three. Finally, my cock couldn't take it anymore, and I convulsed. As I started pumping, Amy opened her eyes. Seeing that I was having an orgasm, she immediately impaled herself and gripped my torso with her thighs. I grabbed her waist and bucked my hips as my balls drained, but she held on like a bull rider, refusing to risk a single drop of my sperm. Like the night before, it was a violent orgasm, and it left me spent. With the last of my spunk deep inside her womb, I released my grip on her waist and let my arms fall to the ground. My heart was racing.

"What should I do?" Amy whispered. Her face was glistening with sweat.

"Just hold still," I said between breaths. "Stay there for a minute."

Amy nodded and hung her head trying to catch her breath too. She seemed pretty exhausted. In the silence of the forest, Amy and I remained still. My mind began to work again as reason returned, and I started to think about Heather.

No doubt Ashley and Heather would be wondering what had happened to us. We had to get back, but I didn't want to ruin Amy's conception chances by having her stand too soon.

"Okay when you are ready," I said. "We will roll together, so you're on your back. Then I'll pull out, okay?"

Amy nodded and smiled. "Thank you, Jake."

It was the first time she had used my name. I touched the side of her face tenderly and noticed her eyes were welling up a little. I could understand her emotions. If everything worked, she would soon have a baby growing inside of her.

"Okay, ready?" I asked.

Amy nodded and together we carefully rolled until she was on her back. I then pulled my cock out, surprised that it was still semi-hard. The moment I was free, she lifted her legs into the air and supported the small of her back with her hands. I had my arms ready in case she teetered, but her balance was good.

"You have great legs," I commented. "Stay like this, and I'll find our clothes. Be right back."

"Take your time, I'm not going anywhere," Amy said quietly.

Once I had found every scattered item, I quickly dressed and then set her clothes aside until she was ready. All she was missing was her boots and spandex pants. They were back wherever Ashley and Heather were waiting – if they were still waiting.

"We need to get back; they're going to start wondering what's up," I said.

"How long should I keep my legs up like this?" Amy asked. "I feel ridiculous."

I glanced at her and admired her legs once more. "I never read the brochure on increasing your chances at conception. Sorry."

"I don't think there is a brochure. This trick could be an old wives tale. Help me please," Amy said. "That was probably enough time. I hope."

"If not, I'm willing to give you a free do-over," I said and laughed when Amy swatted my arm. I steadied her legs as she rolled onto her side and sat up. Picking up her clothes, I offered her a selection of whatever she wanted to put on first. She picked her bra.

"So do you still hate men?" I asked in a teasing voice.

Amy snatched her shirt and slipped it on. "Not all men."

I laughed lightly. "So I won a small victory for men everywhere?"

She raised an eyebrow and snatched her vest. "Don't get ahead of yourself."

"Fair enough," I said. I stood and helped Amy to her feet. During the chase, I hadn't thought to take my bearings, so I didn't know which way we should walk.

"I think it's this way," Amy said as she pointed.

Together we started walking.

I noticed, Amy was trudging through the woods in her bare feet, and I considered offering her my boots, but they were probably way too big for her. Besides, I soon noticed that Amy was very agile. She easily avoided sticks and roots, as she padded along. Maybe she didn't need boots after all. I kept glancing at her slender legs and, of course, stole glances at her perfect little ass whenever I could. I might be married to a stunning woman, but I'm still a man. I can't ignore a beautiful bottom in front of me.

As we wandered around for a while, I began to think we were good and lost. During our game of cat and mouse I didn't think Amy and I had traveled this far, but then again, I could be mistaken. I silently scolded myself for being so careless. As a Marine, I would never have run wildly through the brush without noticing landmarks to help retrace my route. I was getting sloppy in my old age. Then again, I was chasing a half-naked redhead at the time. A man could be forgiven for not taking note of the trees.

Amy saw Heather first and pointed. I followed her gaze and with great relief spotted her too. We angled through the woods watching as Heather paced back and forth. She hadn't seen us yet but as we neared her head turned, and I could see her expression of worry melt away.

"Tell her we're okay," I told Amy.

Sprinting ahead, Amy met up with Heather and the two women hugged. When I arrived, Amy was already in full explanation mode. We had run quite a distance and gotten lost. Heather was holding Amy's spandex pants and boots and handed them over.

"Where's Ashley?" I asked while watching Amy dress.

"She decided to walk up and down the trail to see if she could spot you guys. We were getting worried. Once you two ran out of sight you were gone for a long time," Heather said. "What happened?"

"Sorry about that," I said avoiding her eyes. "Let's go find Ashley."

The Indecent Proposal

I hadn't ridden in a stretch limousine since the day I was married. It's weird, how some memories are jogged by smells, or sights, or even an old song on the radio. As the limo pulled away from the mansion and I watched my husband standing with his hands in his pockets, my memory went back to the day we were married.

If you had told me on my wedding day that I would eventually be working as an escort, I wouldn't have believed you. If you told me on my wedding day that the next time I rode in a limousine, it would be to rendezvous with a well-endowed billionaire for a sex cruise on the lake, I would have thought you crazy, and kicked you out of the car. But here I was, doing just that. Sometimes life is stranger than fiction.

As the car sped me along, I sat back in the comfortable seat and reminisced about how lucky I was to have a husband like Jake. How many husbands were as supportive as he is? Not many. How many husbands would be okay with their wives being escorts? Even less would be my guess.

In retrospect, the ride in the limo which reminded me of my wedding, and then of Jake, actually fortified me against the indecent proposal I was about to receive from Mr. Rutty. But more of that in a little while.

First of all, let me explain the sheer size and opulence of Mr. Rutty's yacht. I've seen big boats in my life. I can tell the difference between a catamaran and a trimaran. I know what a cabin cruiser looks like. I can point out a schooner and a tug boat. But I've never seen a monstrosity like the "boat" Mr. Rutty owned.

My first thought when the limousine stopped at the pier and I stepped out was that there had to be a smaller boat somewhere. There was no way I was taking a tour of the lake in the behemoth moored at the end of the dock.

I was mistaken.

"I hope you enjoy your little adventure, ma'am," the chauffeur said in his adorable French accent. He had set my bag beside me and bowed politely.

"I love your voice, thank you for the lift," I said. He seemed startled and nodded politely before walking back to the car.

I wasn't sure if I was supposed to walk down the dock and get on the giant boat or wait on the shore. I decided to wait and see if Mr. Rutty appeared or perhaps a butler would arrive and escort me aboard the ship. In the meantime, I gazed at his yacht. Now, I'm not very good at judging the size of things. I couldn't tell you how long my limousine was, or how tall a building might be, and I am certainly guessing when I say his boat was over one hundred feet long.

The sides were jet black, which I know is an oddity in the sailing world, as most if not all boats are white. There was a white streak along the side of this ship that broke up the blackness somewhat. All the windows were slanted and tinted black, giving the ship a sleek somewhat menacing appearance. There was a large covered outdoor area in the back of the boat, which, if memory serves, is called the stern. The bow is the pointy part. I knew that much.

As I waited, I wondered how much money a luxury item like that had cost Mr. Rutty. I guess when you're a billionaire, you can afford to splurge a little. Part of me wondered if all this extravagance was his way of showing off, or was he trying to impress me? Normally I would say a man who owns a boat that large was compensating for something, but the memory of Mr. Rutty's gorgeously large cock was still fresh in my mind. Mr. Rutty was not compensating for anything.

I felt a stab of guilt when I thought of Mr. Rutty's cock. Not because he was well endowed, but because I hid the fact he was well endowed from my husband. I also hid my secret desire to feel that giant cock inside of me. I know Jake is okay with me sleeping with clients. There have been very few clients that I ever desired sexually. Mr. Rutty was one of those men. From the moment I saw how well hung he was back in his playroom, I've wanted to feel his thick cock deep inside of me. And I feel guilty for it.

That might be why I didn't react too harshly when Jake said Ashley and her lesbian friends wanted him to impregnate them. Normally I would have lost my mind. There was no way I was about to share my husband's sperm with another woman so she can have his child. But when I stepped back and thought about it, I had to be reasonable. Jake stood by and waited patiently while I slept with many clients. Hell, he even choreographs role playing sessions sometimes, always stepping back so the client can get his rocks off on me. It was only fair that I let him have some fun. I knew he would have refused Ashley's request if I told him no. He respects me that way. Just like I would respect him if he turned down one of my prospective clients. So perhaps, in a way, letting him impregnate those young women, was my way of taking the edge off my guilt at wanting Mr. Rutty to fuck me.

I snapped out of my introspection when the sound of a very throaty car caught my ear. Turning, I looked for the source of the noise. The marina nestled next to the lake, but the access road was a lazy winding descent from higher ground. Any vehicle approaching from the mansion would have to take a series of zigzags to reach the marina.

Sure enough, I spotted a bright red car crest the top of the hill. The engine was high revving and whenever the driver downshifted, the exotic engine roared. I could see it was a Ferarri, though what kind of Ferarri it was eluded me and probably wasn't important. Jake would have known. I watched as it slowly descended the zig zags until it was level with the parking lot. The car then sped up, crossing the parking lot in a blur before gently coming to a stop in a reserved parking spot with a sign above it that read: Mr. Rutty.

I decided he was showing off.

As Mr. Rutty stepped out of his car, I glanced at him over the top of my sunglasses and tried not to laugh. It seemed that Mr. Rutty fancied himself something of a captain. He was regaled in deck shoes, white pants, a dark blue suit jacket with yellow bars around the sleeves, a white dress shirt, and a ridiculous replica navy hat.

I turned away to be polite and focused my attention on the shimmering blue waters of the lake and reminded myself that this man was paying me twenty thousand dollars for my time. I had better not laugh at him.

"Sorry, I'm late. Had some business to take care of," Mr. Rutty said as he walked over to me. "Beautiful day for a sail wouldn't you say?"

I turned and glanced at him and was proud that I didn't giggle. "Yes, it is. I like your car. You should show it to my husband; he loves Hondas."

Mr. Rutty was about to speak when the word 'Honda' registered in his brain and he sputtered and was at a loss for words momentarily. He seemed unable to decide whether or not to explain the virtues of his car or to point out that it wasn't a Honda. I thought my little quip shortened his tail feathers a little.

"Is that your boat?" I asked, averting his attention once more.

"Um, yes. She's a beauty," Mr. Rutty said, somewhat recovered.

I clapped my hands and started towards the dock. Mr. Rutty, noticing my carry-on bag, bent down and scooped it up. He followed quickly, his pace hastened by my enthusiasm.

"How big is your boat?"

"She one hundred and twenty feet. This is my lake boat," Mr. Rutty explained, struggling with the word *boat*. "I have a larger one down in the Bahamas."

"I've never seen a boat so big," I said, making sure not to call it a yacht.

My intention wasn't to be cruel or to make fun of Mr. Rutty. My intention was to subtly show my billionaire client that his treasures and expensive items (like the song says) didn't impress me much. There is nothing worse than a wealthy man full of pride and ego showing off. And in my experience if you build the biggest boat in the world, someone will build one just a tiny bit bigger, or taller, or faster. None of it means anything. I felt it my duty to tone down his expectations of what my reaction would be to such luxuries. Calling his Ferrari a Honda, or his multi-million dollar yacht a boat, was like throwing cold water on the face for a man like Mr. Rutty.

I stopped at the edge of the dock and stared at the massive ship. The practical side of my mind wondered how much it cost to fuel something this big, while the other side of my mind wanted to see the inside.

"Here is your bag, Veronica. Now, if you please, right this way," Mr. Rutty said as he handed me my day bag and gestured towards the walkway leading to the deck. He seemed thoroughly deflated.

I could see crewmembers on board, all dressed in smart white outfits. It made sense to me. A yacht this large would be too much for a single person to captain. You needed people to navigate, pull up the anchor, cook meals, take care of the engine. There was probably a half dozen other tasks I knew nothing about that had to be done to get a ship this big safely underway.

I stood to the side as Mr. Rutty spoke privately with some of the crew. I glanced around the covered open area and admired the fine artistry. Teak wood and polished brass were everywhere in abundance. I wondered how many people could sleep on a boat this size, and imagined that the parties you could throw would be incredible. When Mr. Rutty finished talking, he smiled at me gestured for me to follow him.

"Would you care for a drink? Champaign perhaps?" Mr. Rutty asked as he led me to a full-length bar. There was a smartly dressed young man cleaning glasses who bowed politely and waited for our orders.

"Champaign would be perfect, thank you," I said as I sat on the padded barstool and spun from side to side. It seemed every possible opulent convenience was crammed into the ship.

Mr. Rutty held up two fingers and then turned towards me. He was a persistent man; I'll give him that. The way his eyes looked at me made me feel desired but also a little uncomfortable. He was a man of power and used to getting his way. People obeyed him. I cautioned myself to be careful. A man like Mr. Rutty should be labeled, 'handle with care.'

"How do you like the ship so far?"

"Can I give you a little tip?" I whispered.

Mr. Rutty frowned thoughtfully and then nodded. "Of course. What is it?"

"Lose the hat."

"Pardon?"

"Ditch the captain hat. You look ridiculous," I said quietly.

"But I love this hat."

I winced. "Sorry. It just makes you look old."

That was the magic word. Mr. Rutty did not want to look old. He slipped the hat off his head and set it on the counter, glancing at the bartender who was busy taking the cork out of our champaign bottle before turning back towards me and nodding.

"Better?"

"Now you look handsome," I said reaching up and straightening his hair.

"Thank you."

I put my hand in his and gave him an encouraging squeeze. His face lightened a little, and he rubbed his thumb over my skin. I had to admit it, Mr. Rutty was a handsome man, and he was dangerously polite and charming. I could easily swoon for a man like him. That was the real danger.

I pulled my hand back and tucked it into my lap.

"Your drinks," the bartender said.

I spun on my barstool and picked up my glass. Mr. Rutty picked up his, and we both took a sip. It was delicious, and I didn't want to know what the champaign cost. Bubbles exploded in my mouth.

"Come, I'll give you a quick tour as we get ready to depart," Mr. Rutty said.

That sounded like a great idea. The main floor consisted of luxurious leather couches along the walls and finely polished tables. The recessed lighting made all the brass and stainless steel glimmer and sparkle. Even the carpet under my feet felt soft and spongy, which gave me the sensation of walking on clouds.

An elegant staircase led both up and down and was equipped with more recessed lighting and a highly polished banister. I turned and asked, "Up or down?"

"I'll show you the upper deck first. Nothing too fancy, just the captain's chair and all the navigational stuff. The crew is quite nice," My. Rutty said. "You can meet them."

I took the stairs two at a time like I was an excited little girl with Mr. Rutty close behind. The control room wasn't like anything I expected. Men sat at various stations, and the closest ones looked up when I appeared. Computers and boxes with lights and all sorts of charts and maps felt all very complicated to me, but I did recognize the giant brass wheel.

"Oh, can I sit in the captain's chair? Please? Just for a minute?" I asked.

Mr. Rutty laughed and nodded. "Of course, but don't touch anything."

I bounced across the room, conscious of the appraising eyes of the men. I spun the captain's chair, hopped up, and planted my rump in the seat and smiled at the audience of admirers I had gathered. I kicked my feet back and forth like a little girl and noticed my legs didn't touch the ground. One of the drawbacks of being short, I guess.

Mr. Rutty offered me his hand and helped me down, and I graciously smiled and gave everyone a curtsey. I hoped I was sociable and polite. Even though Mr. Rutty was a client of mine, these crewmen were his employees, and it didn't hurt if I made their boss look more human and boost morale a little.

Next, I was shown the lower galley where I was shocked to see a grand piano and elegant dining tables. Further on was another lounge and in indoor jacuzzi and hot tub. Why not? Past that area was a private deck that overlooked the bow of the ship.

"Where do you sleep?" I asked.

"There are more decks below, young lady. I haven't shown you those rooms yet, or the galley and the crew quarters. If you want, I can take you, but I think we're about to get underway."

I could feel the ship moving and felt the rumble of the engines through my feet. My first thought was wondering where they kept the lifejackets. My second thought was I hope I don't get sea sick.

Mr. Rutty walked out onto the private bow deck and leaned against the railing. I joined him, slipping my arm around his. I could see the limousine still parked beside Mr. Rutty's insulted Ferarri and felt a pang of guilt for mocking him.

As we pulled away from the dock, I looked down at the swirling white foam and beautiful swirling currents of water. I loved the water.

"I was wondering," I said as the ship's bow started to turn towards the open water of the lake.

"Yes?"

"With all these men on board, will we have any privacy?"

He chuckled. "Do you think I would bring a beautiful woman like you on board a ship like this and not have the ability to provide privacy?"

"You seem to be a man of many talents. Is there a place I can freshen up and change into my bikini?" I asked as I finished the last of my champaign and placed the empty glass in his hand.

His eyebrow rose slightly, and he smiled. He walked back into the cabin, and I followed him. He leads me to a change room just off to the side of the jacuzzi and hot tub. I gave him my thanks and slung my bag off my shoulder.

Once inside the changing area, I set my bag down on a teak bench and took a deep breath. The champaign was good, but it was hitting me hard. I opened my bag and pulled out my bathing suit. It wasn't anything fancy, but I liked it's deep green color. It matched my eyes. I quickly undressed and slipped into my bikini. I didn't go for those string bikini bottoms because it felt like you had a constant wedgie. Instead, I liked the small triangle shaped bottoms. They still hinted at what was underneath, but you didn't suffer if you got hungry bum. My bikini top was much less conservative, though. My nipples and areola were covered, but just barely, and I loved the soft green string because it didn't leave a tan line.

With my suit on, I packed my clothes in my bag, pulled out my sunscreen, slipped my sunglasses back on, shouldered my bag, and unlocked the door.

When I returned, Mr. Rutty was standing on the bow gazing out over the blue waters of the lake. There was a constant breeze as the large ship sliced through the waves, but there was barely any rocking motion. I dropped my bag on the deck and joined my wealthy client.

"I'm king of the world!" I cried, holding my arms outwards. At the sound of my voice, Mr. Rutty turned and laughed. I kept my hands stretched outwards to give him the perfect silhouette of my small body. I know my breasts aren't the biggest in the world, but for my frame, they are nice and thick, and I know from behind you can see the sides of them. I strode up to him, wrapped my arms around his neck and gave him an inviting kiss. His hand found the small of my back and then slipped down over my barely covered bum.

I knew he had been patient and it was time to reward him for good behavior. After all, he had spared no expense in his efforts to impress me.

"Do you like my bathing suit?" I asked after I broke our embrace and stepped back. I held my hands together over my head and did a spin for him.

"I like it a lot, but you'll get tan lines," Mr. Rutty said.

"What do you suggest I do?" I asked mischievously.

He thought about it for a moment while looking me over; his dark eyes seemed to flash with mirth. Then he snapped his fingers. "I've got it; you'll have to take everything off. It's the only way to prevent tan lines."

My mouth had made a perfect 'O' before I said, "Are you certain?"

"Yes, and I insist on helping you right this instant," Mr. Rutty declared. He stepped closer and twirled his finger for me to turn around.

I obliged of course and offered him the delicate bow around my neck. I felt his fingers trace my skin lightly and then the slight tension as the tugged the drawstring. He didn't rush or force himself. He simply enjoyed the tiny pleasure of undoing my bikini top. His fingers then slid down my back and pulled the second drawstring. Then warm hands turned me to face him, and I stared into his eyes. His strong jaw set as he leaned closer and kissed me hard. I felt his hand grab the thin fabric of my top and pull it away.

Without pause, he backed me against the tinted windows of the cabin and lifted my hands over my head. His strong grip held my wrists pinned against the glass while his other hand roughly grabbed my breasts. He squeezed and groped before his mouth found mine once more. I found the whole experience thrilling, and I didn't care if the crew could see me or not.

He let go of my wrists, and I began to lower my arms, but he grabbed them again and pressed them against the glass with a warning look. I understood his meaning. When he released them again, I kept them raised. He smiled, satisfied that I was obeying. He stepped back and then knelt on the deck. I watched as his hands found the smaller ties holding my bikini bottoms. He looked up at me and then pulled the tiny strings. I gasped as he slipped his hands under the fabric and slid my bottoms down and then cupped my ass cheeks in his hands.

"Mr. Rutty!" I breathed.

Now I was naked and exposed. He hooked my one leg over his shoulder and without warning pressed his mouth against my already warm pussy. I shuddered in shock. I was not expecting him to do that and my arms splayed across the glass window as I balanced on one leg. I groaned as his experienced mouth, and tongue started to lick and suck my sensitive aroused clit.

"Oh, God, that feels so good," I moaned. It had been so long since anyone ever went down on me, I had forgotten just how pleasurable it was. I shut my eyes and felt the warmth of the sun on my body. His mouth felt so perfect. I fought the urge to grab his head and rub my pussy against his face. That would be unladylike. Whatever magic Mr. Rutty was doing was working because I was soaking wet and hornier than I had been in ages.

When he had his fill, he stood and grabbed my shoulders. I stared into his strong face and determined eyes. His lips glistened with my juices. He bent his neck and kissed me, and I shivered with pleasure. As he kissed, I reached down and fumbled with his pants, yanking and grabbing as fast as I could to get them off. He finally helped, and I freed his enormous cock. I grabbed it with both hands and tugged and jerked it while he continued to kiss me. It was so thick and hard, and I wanted it in my small body so badly.

"Please..." I begged, whispering into his ear. My pleading must have worked because he stopped kissing. Glancing at the railing he half walked and half dragged me to it. He pressed me roughly against the edge, and I peered over the expanse of blue water stretching for what seemed like endless miles. I wrapped my arm around the wood railing to brace myself and felt the cool breeze on my face contrasting with the heat building between my legs.

Mr. Rutty grabbed my small hips and I felt his cock between my legs. I was horny and wet, and his cock slipped into me in one deep thrust. I cried in a mixture of pleasure and pain. His cock was so thick that it filled me and pressed against my sensitive sides. I was overwhelmed with sensations and my knees nearly buckled. His hands gripped my hips even harder, and he started to fuck me. I hung onto the railing, my initial shock of being so roughly entered was replaced with rippling pleasure that my mind couldn't quite process. All I could do was grip the railing as he pounded me roughly.

I had my first creamy orgasm in less than a minute. Maybe it was the fact that the biggest cock I've ever had was deep in my pussy, but I shuddered and trembled and bit my tongue so I wouldn't beg him to stop. He kept ramming and thrusting, his hands like vice grips on my hips. The pressure of his cock crossed all the wires in my brain, but, Mr. Rutty didn't slow or falter his relentless thrusting for several minutes.

Finally, he stopped, pulled out and grabbed my arm, yanking me off the railing. There was a narrow teak bench bolted to the deck which he walked me to. Without saying a word, he forced me face down on the bench and pressed my legs together. My head hung off the end, and I rested my palms on the ground. I wasn't accustomed to being manhandled so roughly. Straddling me, Mr. Rutty spread my ass cheeks and forced the head of his cock back into my swollen pussy. He then leaned forward, pressing his hands on my back to pin me and started to rapid fuck me.

I gasped in shock at first and then I cummed, but he didn't stop. My whole body slammed and bounced on the hard bench with each deep thrust, and his balls hammered the back of my ass and thighs. It was the most intense power fuck I had ever felt and my vision blurred. I began to cry out in pain and pleasure.

I begged him to slow, but he ignored my cries and redoubled his efforts. Orgasms were overlapping each other, and my heart was racing faster than ever. I felt like he was going to split me in half and I wasn't sure how much more my petite body could take of such rough sex. Finally, he grunted and nearly roared as he slammed his cock all the way into me and started to cum. His cock traveled deeper inside of me than anyone had ever been before and I knew he was spurting in the deepest reaches of my womb. When he finished, he nearly collapsed on top of me. Instead, he used the last of his strength to slide his giant cock out of my ruined pussy and stumble off of me.

I had no strength or desire to move and remained on my stomach, shellshocked and limp but in a state of bliss. My head drooped over the edge of the bench, and my eyes were closed. If any of the crew happened to walk by and decide to fuck me, I would have let them. I had no willpower or strength left. How many times had I cummed? More than was probably healthy. I had never been fucked so roughly or so thoroughly in my entire life, and I knew it would take days for my pussy to recover.

"Come over here," Mr. Rutty said with some effort.

I turned my head and looked at him. He was lying on a very comfortable looking recliner; his spent cock flopped across his thigh. My god, I thought, his cock was huge. I couldn't believe that thing fucked me.

He motioned me to come. Reluctantly I forced my body off the bench and sat up. My pussy felt warm and gushy and stretched. I took a few breaths then got to my feet and walked over to his recliner and climbed half on and half beside him. I rested my head on his strong shoulder and placed my hand on his chest. I could feel his heart still beating quickly. He put his arm around me and stroked my arm.

Neither of us spoke. We just listened to the thrum of the engine and the occasional cry of a seagull. The sun was bright, and the sky was blue, and the wind was perfect. The gentle motion of the boat soon lulled me to sleep.

I think I was smiling.

Strange Confessions

Heather wasn't amused when she found out that Amy and I spontaneously had sex in the woods. We tried to apologize and explain that it just happened. I took full responsibility, telling Heather that I let the magic of the moment get the better of me and reassuring her that she will be next.

"But I always wanted to play out the whole lady in distress being rescued fantasy," Heather pouted. "I got dressed up for nothing."

Trying to make the best of the situation, I tried to make Heather see the bright side. "You should be happy for your friend. Unplanned and spontaneous, passionate sex increases the chances of conception by at least fifty percent."

"Really?" Heather asked.

I had no idea. I just made that number up. The point is, Amy and I had hot passionate animal sex in the middle of the woods, and if that didn't get her pregnant, then I don't know what will.

"Cheer up," I said, putting my arm around her. "I'm a man of my word. I've hopefully gotten your two best friends pregnant. Do you think I'm so heartless that I wouldn't do everything in my power to help you too?"

Heather tried to smile, but I could still see the disappointment on her face.

"Tell you what," I said, trying to comfort her. "You said you have a damsel in distress being rescued fantasy, well, how about a kidnapped by a villain and forced to have sex fantasy? I know lots of women who get off on that."

"You mean a rape fantasy?" Heather asked with a hint of disdain.

"Along those lines," I said reading her tone. "Nothing violent or painful. Just role playing. You could be the helpless beautiful victim, and I'm the stalker maybe. I kidnap you and take you to my secret lair where I tie you up and force you to do things against your will."

"What sort of things?"

"Well, whatever you want. It would be your fantasy," I said.

Heather was quiet for a moment. "Let me think about it."

I nodded, not wanting to force her to try something she wasn't comfortable with. Even though some women harbored secret rape fantasies, it didn't mean Heather did. For all I knew, maybe she wanted to reverse the role and kidnap me. Whatever she decided, I would do my best to accommodate her desires.

We found Ashley on the trail, and after a short explanation, with Ashley rolling her eyes at Amy, we all decided to head back to the mansion to shower and clean up. Heather and Amy would ride back on horses, while Ashley and I would find our stashed dirtbike and ride back together. As Ashley and I turned to walk up the trail, Amy called me. I turned and looked at her. She wanted a moment to me, so I told Ashley to go on ahead. She nodded and kept going.

"What is it?" I asked as I approached Amy. "Is everything okay?"

Amy glanced over her shoulder. Heather was already making her way to the horses that were tied in a small clearing. No one would overhear us.

"I just wanted to thank you," Amy said with sincerity in her voice.

I put my hands on her shoulders. "There is no need for that Amy. It was an honor for me. I'm the one who should thank you for the privilege."

Her blue eyes searched my face for a moment. "Honor? Why?"

"I'm a married man, Amy. Though I want to start a family of my own, I'm not sure when that will happen, if it happens at all. To me, being asked to father children for you, beautiful young women is a huge honor. I just hope I can give you strong, healthy children, and I envy the happy lives you will all have."

Amy tilted her head. "You mean that. I can see it in your eyes."

"I do mean it. I know I've just met you three, but I can see the love you have for each other and that closeness is rare. You are all great girls, and you are all going to be great mothers too. Your children will give you that common bond that will keep you together. Trust me; this is a huge honor for me, so I'm the one who should be saying thank you."

"Thank you for showing me not all men are jerks."

"Well, I don't know about that," I said in jest. I gave Amy a hug, and she returned it. For a moment we stood in the stillness of the forest.

"I will always remember this day," Amy said and sniffled.

I smiled at her and kissed her on the forehead, then brushed a tear from her cheek. If I weren't married and so in love with Veronica, then I would have chosen someone like Amy. I admired her fierce spirit. There was something about her that was different, and I was drawn to it.

"You are going to be a great mom. Keep in touch if you want."

"I'd like that," Amy said. "I think my child should know what a great man their father is."

"I have to go," I said quietly. My eyes stung a little, and I felt a lump in my throat. Stepping back, I nodded proudly. Amy clasped her hands in front of her and watched me. Slowly a small smile lifted the corners of her mouth, and she turned, and without looking back, hurried to catch up to Heather.

I knew I would miss Amy, and watched her bound through the trees to catch up with her friend. I turned and walked up the trail. Ashley would be waiting. I liked her too. Damn, this was hard. I had to figure out how to keep my emotions out of my work. How does Veronica do it? Toughen up, Jake; I admonished myself. You were hired to do a job. That's it.

By the time I caught up with Ashley, I was my old self again.

Unfinished Business

I woke from my peaceful nap when Mr. Rutty slipped out of the recliner and stood. Rolling my naked body over, I shielded my eyes from the bright sun and smiled at him and then glanced at his still impressive cock as it hung limp. My god, I wished Jake had a cock like that.

"How long did we sleep?" I asked. I arched my back, thrusting my bare breasts outward as I stretched and sat up. My pussy was sore, but I ignored the discomfort.

"About an hour," Mr. Rutty said. He moved to the railing and looked out over the water, his naked profile filling my head with impure thoughts once more. He turned, and my eyes ignored his dangling cock. "We're nearing Peter's Point. You can see the old lighthouse. We'll start circling back any minute now. Did you sleep well?"

"I did," I said. I stood and joined Mr. Rutty at the railing. "For some reason, I was relaxed. I've never been shagged like that before."

He glanced at me and said, "Really?"

I snuggled into his side and giggled. "Mr. Rutty, you have the biggest cock I have ever seen. You got a little carried away. I'm a little sore."

"I'm sorry, I tried to contain myself, but there is something about you Veronica. I can't put my finger on it. You make me feel young again."

"Well I'm glad you enjoyed my company," I said. Even though Mr. Rutty was an older man, he was rugged and handsome, and I liked his refined manners.

He put his arm around my shoulder and drew me between him and the railing. I fit perfectly between his arms. I felt his body press against my back as his hands cupped my breasts. I felt warm and peered out over the lake.

"I had a chat with my nephew this morning," Mr. Rutty suddenly said.

I tensed for a second, wondering if I was going to be scolded or not. I looked up. "Oh really? And how is he?"

"Not in a good mood," Mr. Rutty said quietly. "The cleaning staff found him handcuffed to his bed. Apparently, he spent the night like that."

"How strange," I said. "Somebody must have forgotten to unlock him."

"He's gone home back to Texas. That's why I was late meeting you at the docks. He seemed to be in a hurry, and I drove him to the airport."

"I wonder what could have sent him packing so quickly?"

Mr. Rutty chuckled. "I think I have a pretty good idea," he said giving my tit a squeeze and leaning into my back.

"Are you upset?" I asked after a moment. My tits were his to play with. He continued to caress my breasts, his warm hands giving me pleasure. I thought he hadn't heard me, but he finally sighed.

"Can I be honest with you, Veronica?"

"Always, Darling."

"I don't care much for Steven. I never did, and quite frankly it bothered me to think about you helping him with his rite of passage. He doesn't deserve such a beautiful woman. He is too young to appreciate someone like you. If I knew what kind of woman you were, I would have refused his request. I'm sorry you had to experience whatever happened between you two."

"Mr. Rutty, if I didn't know better, I'd think you cared for me."

He turned me around in his arms. His face was earnest and his eyes filled with passion. I had seen that look before, and I braced myself.

"Stay with me," Mr. Rutty begged.

"Pardon?"

"Stay with me. Divorce your husband and marry me. I need you."

"Mr. Rutty, please," I said pushing him back to get some breathing room. "You don't even know me. I'm married, and I love my husband very much."

I could see his determined jaw clench in frustration. His eyes pleaded. He thought he loved me, but it was just lust. He loved my body. Despite how much I liked him, I wasn't about to throw away what my husband and I had.

"Can I hire you?"

"You already have, Mr. Rutty."

"No, I mean to be my personal assistant. With benefits. I will pay you whatever you want. Stop being an escort and come work for me. You can live in the mansion—"

I put my hand on his lips. "You aren't the first man to profess his love for me, but I have, to be honest with you Mr. Rutty. You don't love me. You just think you do. Please don't make this awkward, okay?"

He took a deep breath and looked away. "I'm a man used to getting his way. What is it you want? Jewelry? A car? I can whisk you away to anyplace in the world. We can dine in Venice, or eat the finest caviar on the shores of the Caspian. I can give you anything you desire. Just be with me."

I felt sad for Mr. Rutty. I saw a man who had everything in life except the one thing that would make him truly happy; love. He was offering me the very things that didn't make him happy, in exchange for the one thing that did.

"I love my husband. I'm sorry, Mr. Rutty. I'm very fond of you, but I don't love you any more than you love me. What we've done together, as mind blowing as it was, is not love."

Hanging his head, Mr. Rutty nodded. "I know. I just hoped in time we could grow to love each other. What does your husband have that I could not give you?"

I touched his arm, and he looked at me. "It's in here," I said pointing to my chest. "That's something no amount of money can buy."

He remained silent for a while and then nodded. "You're right. I'm sorry."

"Now, let's go inside and enjoy that jacuzzi. Then you can make me something to eat. I'm starving."

"I can see how easily men fall in love with you, Veronica."

"You can?"

"You have a zest for life that is contagious. You light up a room when you enter. Your eyes they sparkle. You are fresh air and sunshine for the soul."

"Plus I look good naked.

Mr. Rutty laughed. "Yes, that too. Your husband is a lucky man."

"Yes, he is. Now that all that is settled. Let's soak in the jacuzzi and then you can make me a sandwich."

"Oh, can I?" He said.

"Yes. And I'm craving pickles," I said as I spun away and strolled towards the cabin door. I could see his reflection in the tinted window. It was good to see him laughing.

* * *

I found Ashley leaning against the dirtbike in the little clearing. I didn't want to talk. I was thinking about Amy and how feisty she was and how much her personality and mannerisms matched Veronica's own.

"I wish we could fuck one more time," Ashley said.

I nearly stumbled over my own feet. "What?"

"I said I wish you could fuck me one more time before you go."

I looked around the clearing as I approached her. "Is this because you want to be sure you're pregnant or because I'm such an amazing lover you just can't get enough of me?"

Ashley laughed. "You aren't like other men I know."

"How many men do you know?" I rested against the bike and folded my arms. I had discarded my torn fluffy shirt and wondered if my naked torso was turning her on. A man can hope, can't he?

"Plenty, but not in the way you're thinking. I told you already; I like girls."

"I hear that a lot lately," I mused. "You're an odd girl, Ashley."

"In what way?" she asked, as stood only inches away and dug her hands into my front pockets. She regarded me with impenetrable eyes.

"You start the conversation, not with how was your day, but with how much you want to fuck. And then almost immediately you remind me that you like girls." I scratched my chin. "How am I supposed to process that?"

Ashley giggled. "I'm complicated. You need to figure it out."

I wrapped my arms around her slender waist and pulled her closer. She leaned her head forward, and I found her warm, soft lips kissing mine. Damn she was a good kisser. I recalled the previous night when I got a line of blowjobs; it was Ashley who felt the best.

"You're getting hard," Ashley observed.

I spun her around roughly, and she gasped as I grabbed her heavy breasts and squeezed them through her elven top. I then turned her sideways and ran my hand over her ass and cupped her ass cheeks. She responded by closing her eyes and making soft sounds.

"We can't," I said, pulling my hands away. "I'm saving it for Heather. I feel really bad she got all dressed up and ready, and I fucked Amy instead. I should have stuck with the plan."

Ashley turned to face me, her mouth pouty. "We all got dressed up. I can't believe you just took her like that in the middle of the forest and fucked her brains out. It's so romantic."

She leaned against me. My hands slid over her very fine ass once more. I squeezed her butt cheeks and felt my cock straining in my pants. My thoughts began to get fuzzy. I wanted to tear her clothes off and bend her over the bike and ram my cock up her ass, but that wouldn't be very professional. I had to save my stamina for Heather.

"You know, after this weekend, we can be secret fuck buddies," Ashley whispered into my ear. The revelation shocked me.

"What do you mean?"

"You know. When I need that cock of yours, you come over and fuck me silly. I could pay you each time. Hell, a man like you could go into business as a call guy. Lots of women would pay for a big buff Marine to fuck them."

I hadn't considered that.

She must have seen the gears in my head spinning, and she laughed. "Don't get full of yourself stud," Ashley teased. "I was only joking. Seriously, though, I want you to fuck me again. I need it now, and I'm going to need it before I get married. Hell, if we can pull it off, you can fuck me in my wedding dress."

I frowned. "I don't like wearing dresses. Besides, you come from a powerful family, and I'm not going to make enemies like that no matter how much I want to fuck you. I want to be fair to your friend."

"Fine," Ashley said. "Can I suck your cock?"

"Oh my god I want to say yes," I said in frustration. "But no. Come on; let's get back before I change my mind. Damnit, you got me all hard again. Fuck!"

My consternation only made Ashley laugh. She pulled away, but her eyes were full of desire. She watched me prime and set the choke on the bike. I channeled my sexual frustration into the kick starter, and the bike fired up on the first try.

I revved the engine and motioned for Ashley to climb on. Without a shirt, I felt like some romantic hero riding a steel horse with a gorgeous woman on the back. If Veronica saw me now, I'm sure she would have some questions. It wasn't my fault that the fluffy shirt was poorly made or that Amy had torn my shirt off my body so we could have animal sex.

It would be better if I got back to the mansion before she finished her cruise, though. I flicked the bike into gear and adjusted my cock so it wouldn't break while I rode, then pulled out onto the trail. Ashley snuggled into my back, and her hand slipped over my crotch and massaged my cock while I rode.

The entire way back to the stables, I fought the urge to pull over and fuck her.

The Long Ride Home

When Veronica and Mr. Rutty returned to the mansion, I had already had a hot shower and was relaxing, comfortable on her bed. She came in quietly, dropped her bag on the floor and jumping into bed beside me.

"You got some sun today," I said. She smelled like fresh air.

"I'm so tired!" Veronica said into her pillow. She reached up with her hands and started to undo her braided hair, but gave up part way through and went limp.

I poked her side. "Hey, no sleeping!"

"I can sleep if I want to." Veronica pouted.

Leaning over, I unbraided the rest of her hair. Veronica smiled, but her eyes stayed closed. Sitting up, I rolled out of bed and took off her sandals. Then I pulled her shorts off, admiring her tiny round ass briefly, before helping her sit up.

"Arm up," I said and pulled her sleeve off. She offered her other arm next, and I tugged her top the rest of the way off. She was wearing her white lace panties and bra. I looked at my wife, her hair all disheveled and her smooth skin slightly tanned and felt my cock respond.

"Did you and Mr. Rutty have a nice cruise?"

Veronica nodded, and I noted the small smile that crept across her face. I had little doubt my wife would have enjoyed herself. She always loved the water. I was smart enough not to ask about the sex part. She was an escort, and he did pay us a hell of a lot of money. Sometimes it's better not to know the details.

"Did you get those girls pregnant yet?" Veronica asked in a sleepy voice.

"Almost. One down, and one more to go," I said.

"Which one was it?"

"Amy. The red head."

"Oh, nice. She's a cute girl. Great butt. Was she fun?"

"I didn't last long," I said. It was the truth.

Veronica laughed and rolled onto her side, snuggling her head into her pillow and tucking her hands under her cheek. "You never do."

"I'll have to arrange a time and place for Heather's turn. I feel bad leaving her for last," I said absently, not sure if Veronica was still with me. I unfolded a bedspread and gently draped it over my wife. She mumbled something I couldn't understand. She was quickly drifting. Too much sunshine and fresh air had taken the wind out of her sails. My wife was like the Energizer Bunny, but when her batteries die, she crashes like a brick.

I leaned close and kissed her on the cheek.

"I wuv you," Veronica whispered. I liked it when she used funny words.

Patting her hip gently, I grabbed my room key and quietly left. I'd let her sleep for a bit while I checked with Ashley and the girls. Maybe Heather had an idea or fantasy she wanted to role play, or maybe she just wanted a straight up shag. I would have preferred a little role playing, just to help me stay hard. At my age, I find having sex more than once a day, sometimes a little tricky. Not that I'd admit that to anyone, and before you ask, no I don't take any of those stupid male enhancement supplements. Those are for old guys.

I was starting to learn my way around the mansion pretty well. It was still a massive place with more rooms and hallways than you could shake a stick at, but I had learned the route to Ashley's elevator at least.

As I waited for the doors to open, I marveled at the absurdity of our weekend adventure. My wife was hired to help take the virginity of a college kid who turned out to be one of her former students all grown up while I ended up being paid to impregnate three rich lesbians, one of whom is about to marry the very college kid my wife is here to bang. I chuckled to myself. Life is stranger than fiction.

The elevator doors opened, and I stepped inside and pressed the button. Part of me was a little sad that my wife and I would be leaving in the morning. I had grown to like Ashley and Amy and even the wild and crazy

Heather. I hadn't gotten to know Mr. Rutty, but my wife liked him and she was a good judge of character. The one person I didn't want to meet was his nephew, Steven Rutty. So far I hadn't run into the kid, and as far as I was concerned, that was fine by me.

I arrived at Ashley's apartment to find all three of the girls wearing skimpy lingerie sleeping in Ashley's pink bed. I stood in the doorway and scratched my head at the tangle of arms and legs, breasts and asses. Should I wake them or let them sleep?

Not sure what to do, I slowly backed out of her bedroom and walked over to the living room couch and plopped myself down. I could go back to my room, and nap or I could go to my wife's room and wake her up. Or I could let her sleep, but then why would I go to her room? Or, I could stay here and try to wake Heather or one of the other girls. On the other hand, I could simply sit on this comfy couch and wait. Why was everyone so bloody tired all of the sudden?

Remembering the motto; discretion is the better part of valor, I folded my arms and waited. If nothing else, a little peace and quiet were just what I needed. Then I started to think. Weren't we all supposed to be back at the mansion around five to have supper? I looked at my watch. It was nearly five-thirty, and I was hungry.

Why were Ashley, Amy and Heather all wearing lingerie at this time of the day? I assumed once we got back that they would have showered and changed like I

110

had and then met up for dinner. Instead, it looked like they showered and decided to put on sexy outfits and have an impromptu slumber party. I wondered if they had a little threesome lesbian makeout session. According to Ashley, they had all been friends since college and did "everything" together. Including having children it seemed. I imagined the three of them all naked and kissing each other. That would be so hot to watch.

Well, I had to try and impregnate Heather still. She had been more than understanding considering I ruined her 'fantasy in the woods' idea by shagging Amy instead of her. I owed Heather a special session at the very least. And I had to complete my task before Veronica, and I left in the morning.

I returned to Ashley's bedroom and peered in again. None of the girls had moved. I had half a mind to slip into bed with them all and slowly seduce Heather while her friends slept. I could fuck her right there on the bed, I thought.

Then I blinked. Well, why the hell don't I? What was the worst thing that could happen? Ashley and Amy wake up and join in? A grin spread across my face as I quietly stripped naked and approached the bed. My cock was eagerly growing as I gazed at slender legs and smooth stomachs. Amy's face was nearest the edge of the bed, her shoulder length red hair still damp from the shower. I stood over her, my cock only inches from her face and gently stroked myself. I could cum all over her;

111

I thought and be done before she even woke. Ashley was on her stomach, her legs parted and her baby blue lingerie bottoms flared just enough that I could see the curve of her ass cheeks and the smooth, sensual lines of her tight pussy. She was a great fuck and to think she was begging me earlier to do her again. Oh to be a young man again and be able to fuck five times a day.

I finally gazed at Heather. She wore a sheer pink top and panties; her wild blonde hair was all over the place as usual. She was on the other side of the bed. I carefully made my way around and knelt beside the bed and gazed at her sleeping body. Of the three girls, I knew the least about Heather and felt she got short changed. When she gave me a blowjob the other night, I could tell she wanted to do more, but I moved on. And today, I ruined her fantasy.

I was going to make it up to her. I gently ran my fingers up her leg, feeling her tight skin. Heather had nice legs, and I could tell she was either a cyclist or ice skater because of her muscle tone. I gently caressed her thigh and then switched to the back of my hand and gently brushed her arm. She stirred a little in her sleep, and I waited.

When I was sure she still sleeping, I slowly slipped my hand into her sheer panties. Her pussy lips were tight, and her skin was firm. I rubbed my finger up and down, slowly working it between her folds until I found her clit.

She moved a little and turned her head, but remained sleeping.

I smiled and continued to make tiny circles with my fingers. Little by little Heather's body responded. Then she moaned ever so softly in her sleep and parted her legs a few inches. I kept rubbing and caressing until her hips started to respond with small movements. She grew wetter, and I could tell my seduction was working.

Risking exposure, I tugged and slipped her panties down. She rocked her hips from side to side while she slept, either consciously or not, allowing me to slip her panties completely off. Now with her clothing out of the way, I gently spread her legs a little. Heather obliged my gentle prodding by opened her legs more. I slipped my arms under her thighs, carefully lifting her bottom off the bed and drawing her pussy towards me.

As gently as I could, I bent her knees back and pushed them apart. Her beautiful pussy opened like a flower, and I gazed at her shaven pink skin in awe. I kissed her soft, creamy inner thigh, working my mouth steadily closer to her clit while holding her bent legs apart. I could smell her freshness and see her wet juices already starting to soak her folds.

I was tempted to ram my cock into her right away. But I wanted to make this special, and I wanted to taste her pussy. I sucked and licked her labia softly, getting it wet with my mouth while slowly rubbing her clit with my finger. She was responding now, and I knew if I didn't start sucking her clit, she would wake up.

Pressing my lips on her nub, I nibbled and then kissed it. Then I opened my mouth and began to massage it with my tongue. I could feel the nub working around and around in my mouth. She moaned, and her hips pivoted to give me better access. I tasted her, and she was sweet. Her stomach muscles convulsed and I could hear Heather starting to breath quicker. She turned her head and ran a hand through her hair, but she still seemed to be sleeping. I bet she was having the best dream right now.

I kept working, slowly warming her up and giving her a small climax. A tiny gasp from her mouth alerted me that I was making progress. I kept my rhythm and kept licking and twirling my tongue making sure not to use too much pressure or rush her. Her hand slipped between her legs and found my mouth and then her fingers worked up the side of my face and gripped my hair. I could feel her gently guide my efforts, and I felt encouraged.

Heather opened her eyes and glanced down at me. I kept licking and sucking and peered up at her startled face and winked. Her shock melted into disbelief as she glanced at her two sleeping friends and then back at me. She covered her mouth briefly and then gave me a silent oh my god scream. I nodded and kept working my mouth. Her eyes became sharp, and she sucked in her breath and bit her lip. She started to convulse, her tight stomach muscles working. She gripped the bed sheets and stifled a cry. I watched her tilt her head back and silently scream as her pussy twitched and convulsed and she cummed. I felt the gush and was shocked by it. She straightened her legs and wrapped them around my shoulders and ground her pussy into my face. I redoubled my efforts and got a face full of warm juices as my reward. As her orgasm subsided her legs went limp, and her grip on my hair loosened into a caressing thank you. She offered me her hand, and I helped her sit up. She hugged me and suppressed happy laughter and then looked into my eyes.

"You're welcome," I silently mouthed.

Heather snorted and covered her face. Her breathing was still ragged and then she noticed my hard cock and went still. Slowly she lifted her chin and looked at me with a question on her face. I nodded and kissed her. I could see the flush on her cheeks as she understood what I meant.

"Where?" Heather mouthed.

I nodded towards the bed we were on, and her eyes drew wide.

"My friends are sleeping!" she mouthed again. I was enjoying our silent conversation and shrugged.

Her expression said, "Really?"

I nodded, and Heather bit her lip. She considered for a moment and then threw caution to the wind and agreed.

Standing, I moved closer while Heather leaned back on her elbows and spread her legs. She reached for her clit with both hands and in the process pressed her firm breasts together with her arms. She stared at me in wonder as she rubbed her clit and waited.

I grabbed my cock and gently prodded her wet pussy. She was ready and closed her eyes. I slipped the head in and then gently let my cock sink into her. Heather turned her head to the side and squeezed her eyes shut as my cock filled her. She was just as tight as Ashley and Amy and her pussy gripped my shaft like a glove. It became obvious to me at that moment that none of the three girls had ever had a lot of sex with guys. As a result, they were all nubile and tight.

I bent down and sucked both her nipples as I slowly drew my cock out and then slid it back in. I didn't want to cause her discomfort. She was so tight that I wasn't going to last long anyway. Heather touched the side of my face with her hand, and I kissed her fingers as I slowly increased my hip thrusts.

Amy rolled over and opened her eyes. She smiled at me and then blinked away her sleep and sat up. It only took a second for her to realize that I was fucking Heather and she grinned.

"Oh my God, it's happening!" Amy said as she shook Ashley violently.

I laughed. There goes my plan of secretly impregnating Heather.

"Hello, Amy," I said. "Well, we might as well make noise now."

"I can't believe you snuck in here to fuck her like that. That's so romantic!"

I looked at Amy and snickered. It was hardly romantic. Borderline creepy, but not romantic, unless Heather was my wife.

Ashley sat up and rubbed her eyes. "Are you fucking her on my bed?"

"I am if that's okay with you," I said, increasing my tempo. The bed began to bounce now and Heather, though she was trying to say something, was at a loss for words. She covered her mouth as another orgasm came and she squeezed her eyes shut.

"I think the whore likes it!" Amy said in jest. She looked slightly envious.

Heather giggled and nodded her head. "I am, damn it. It feels good!"

"This is my last hurrah ladies," I said without slowing my pace. "Could you two do me one last favor before I impregnate your friend?"

Ashley and Amy looked at each other and nodded.

"Give me a strip tease," I said.

Amy giggled and shook her head. "Why should we?"

"Because I want to have the biggest orgasm of my life and I want to see your cute tits jiggling and bouncing while I cum inside Heather."

Ashley relented and peeled off her top. I humped Heather harder, my eyes glued to Ashley's big thick breasts. Not to be outdone, Amy peeled off her top and her bottoms too. Her breasts weren't as large, but she made up for it by turning around and giving me a great view of her gorgeous ass cheeks.

That was all I needed. I grunted and humped Heather harder, slamming my cock home without thought now. I just wanted to cum as hard and as deep as I could. Sweat formed on my brow. I gritted my teeth, tensed my muscles and then exploded deep inside Heather's pussy. I bent her legs back, almost bending her in half so my cock could find the deepest most fertile part of her womb. I gave her everything I could muster, grunting and pumping until every last drop squirted deep inside her. Covered in sweat, I released her legs and rolled to the side, collapsing on the bed.

Ashley was there right away and gripped Heather's ankles. "Quick get your arse up in the air and hold your legs up."

I laughed at the sight of the blonde trying to balance Heather's legs on the shifting rocking bed. I looked at

Amy, and we made eye contact. Nodding towards the door, I got out of bed, and Amy followed me.

"We'll leave you two alone for a few minutes," I said.

Amy handed me my clothes and then reached for my hand. We walked into the living room and sat down on the couch. I unfolded my shirt and slipped it on.

"I'm going to miss you," Amy said, her blue eyes turning serious. "Can I ride you one more time before you go?"

I shook my head. "I have to be honest, Amy. You were the most fun out of all of them. I mean it," I said as I pulled my boxers up.

Amy blushed and nodded, her hand squeezing my own. "Thank you. Of all the men I've slept with I guess I can honestly say you were the best."

"If I can ever talk my wife into having a threesome, would you ever consider joining us?" I asked. I stood and put on my shorts.

"Was that why you brought me out here? To see if I'll sleep with you and your wife in the future?"

I loved her fiery spirit. "No, I came out to tell you that I'm going to miss you the most and to wish you the best. If I wasn't married and I was twenty years younger, I would chase you down until eventually you relented and let me marry you."

Amy laughed and watched as I slipped my sandles on. "If you weren't married, you wouldn't have to be twenty years younger. I'd accept right now."

"You would?" I looked up.

"You are a handsome man and an ex-soldier, but you are a slow learner, Jake. Your wife is a lucky woman, and I'm a lucky woman. Thank you for what you've done for the three of us. I had planned on never getting married to a man. I hated men, but you've ruined all that. I want your baby more than anything in the world, Mr. Miller and I will always remember you."

"Well, I guess that just about sums it all up," I said. Amy had given me a lot to think about.

"Go back to your wife. One of us will be in touch and keep you updated," Amy said. She stood, and I gazed at her naked body. I ran my hand up her legs and over her perfectly round ass, then up the small of her back and across the front until I found her perky breast. She smiled when I rolled her tiny nipple and pulled my hand away.

"Give everyone my best," I said.

"I'll walk you to the elevator."

"Shouldn't you put clothes on?"

"I want you to remember me like this. Before I get fat." She took my hand rubbed her flat stomach for good luck. We walked silently towards the elevators.

"I liked your ass a lot," I confessed.

Amy chuckled. "I liked your cock."

I turned and cupped her face in my hands and then leaned down and kissed her softly. I had to get away. I was not a professional escort, and my feelings were getting too stirred. I stepped back, glanced at her slender naked body once more and then stepped into the elevator.

I stood and silently looked at Amy until the elevator doors closed and took me down. When I stepped out, I quietly walked back to my wife's room and unlocked the door. She was still sleeping when I stepped inside. I gently closed the door behind me and checked on her. She was so beautiful.

I took a quick shower and then climbed into bed beside Veronica. For some reason, I felt guilty. My wife snuggled into me, but she didn't wake. I knew she was exhausted. I stared at the ceiling for a long time, processing my thoughts.

We would pack up in the morning and say our goodbyes. I wasn't sure if I would see Ashley or Heather or Amy in the morning. I didn't even want to see Mr. Rutty, but I guessed it was only polite to thank our client.

Then Veronica and I would get into my car, and we would make the long drive home and back to our lives once more. I'd check the phone messages, and Veronica would check our emails.

In a day or two, the cheque would clear, and we'd pay off the mortgage. In the meantime, I guess Veronica and

I will start searching travel websites to find a nice long cruise. I wanted to go somewhere tropical.

Veronica needed a vacation. As I drifted off to sleep, with my wife snuggling into me, I smiled. I needed a vacation too.

The End

The JJ Stuart Catalogue

Jake & Robin: The Wife Slave Series

Decided
Broken.
Revenged
Also available as a complete Trilogy

Katie's Mom Series

Watching Katie's Mom
Caught by Katie's Mom
Punished by Katie's Mom
Shared by Katie's Mom
Also available as a complete Series

Down the Dark Path Trilogy

A Cheating Wife's Journey from Innocence to Submission

Book 1. **The Fall of Julie Snow**
Book 2. **The Training of Julie Snow**
Book 3. The Demise of Julie Snow
Also available as a complete Trilogy

My Wife The Kinky Escort

Book 1. Hired By Her Co-Worker
Book 2. Rite of Passage

Stand Alone Sizzling Quick Reads

The Dominant Wife
Femdom, male chastity cuckold!

Love on the Beach
A secret rendezvous leads to a torrid love affair with a hot wife!

A Romp in the Gym
A late night encounter with an ex might solve her fertility problems!

Tara's First Time Tied
Can she handle her first BDSM sex with her secret lover?

Thank you for all your support and feedback. Feel free to send me an email or sign up for my discreet mailing list, or if you have story ideas you would like to suggest and see in print, drop me a line. I'd be glad to hear from you!

J.J.Stuart@hotmail.com

Printed in Great Britain
by Amazon

27737073R00069